WITHIN THESE WALLS

When Annie revisits Chattelcombe Priory, it's inevitable that unwelcome memories are stirred. It's where she'd fallen in love with Edward, and where Charlotte's accident, which changed everything, had happened. When Edward returns to buy the Priory, he also attempts to win back Annie. But Tim, the vicar, wants to turn the Priory into a retreat centre, and Annie finds herself torn between the two men. Then, she discovers a secret, which changes her perception of the past . . .

Books by Susan Sarapuk
in the Linford Romance Library:

COMING HOME

SUSAN SARAPUK

◆

WITHIN
THESE WALLS

Complete and Unabridged

LINFORD
Leicester

First published in Great Britain in 2010

First Linford Edition
published 2011

British Library CIP Data

Sarapuk, Susan.
  Within these walls.- -
  (Linford romance library)
  1. Love stories.
  2. Large type books.
  I. Title II. Series
  823.9′2–dc22

  ISBN 978–1–4448–0768–4

Published by
F. A. Thorpe (Publishing)
Anstey, Leicestershire

Set by Words & Graphics Ltd.
Anstey, Leicestershire
Printed and bound in Great Britain by
T. J. International Ltd., Padstow, Cornwall

This book is printed on acid-free paper

1

She'd had the dream again last night. Annie Anson sat at the kitchen table in her mother's house, cradling a mug of tea in her hands, and stared unseeing at the window. Maybe it was because she'd come home that events of her childhood seemed so vivid.

There they were again, the three of them — Edward, Charlotte, herself — she and Edward, partners in adventure, running away from his sister, hiding amongst the ruins of The Old Priory. Charlotte catching up with them because Edward allowed her to — it was part of the game. Charlotte, threatening to tell their father and Edward, panicking, pushing her. Charlotte losing her footing tumbling from the uneven steps onto the hard ground below, coming to rest like a broken china doll, whimpering. Annie had never been able to erase the sound of her friend's whimpers.

She screwed up her eyes now and shook her head as if that would loosen the image from her memory. It had all happened so long ago. Put it away, forget about it. There were things that needed to be done. She had a funeral to arrange.

* * *

'Annie, so sorry to hear about your mother.'

'Thank you,' Annie said as she paid for her newspaper. She remembered Tom, the newsagent; he'd been in the village forever.

'You're looking well. How's work? Are you still in New York?'

'Still there. Work's fine, everything's good.'

He gave her a kindly smile.

'There've been a lot of changes since you left here. For you I mean, not for me. People like me stay here for years.

Have you heard that The Priory's up for sale?'

'No, I hadn't. That's interesting. Well, I'd better be off. Things to arrange.' She paid for her newspaper and escaped. That's how she'd felt all those years ago — the overwhelming need to escape this place, her history and her mother. Well, one of them was gone now; the others she sensed she would never outrun.

Annie hurried along the road hoping she wouldn't meet anybody, until she came to the first house in the village standing next to the roadsign which read: 'Chattelcombe'. A white building with a central front door painted a bottle green and windows either side, the house still had the ability to stir up mixed feelings — memories of happy early years when her father was still alive followed by her increasingly fraught later childhood and teenage years kicking against her mother's desires and attempts to dictate her life.

Yet despite all that, she was sorry her

mother was gone. She'd tried hard the past few years to make things better between them, but it had been just so difficult.

'I would never have made the choices you did,' her mother had said ascerbically the last time Annie had invited her out to New York, eighteen months ago.

Annie had smiled and let it go; you couldn't live another person's life for them. She was happy with the choices she'd made.

She'd been out on a job at Long Island when the call had come nearly two weeks ago.

'There was a call from a Val Linton,' Jessica, her flatmate had said as she'd come in at the end of the day and dumped her bags and equipment on the hall floor. 'I tried to reach you but your cell was off. She's left a number for you to ring back.'

Annie had guessed it was bad news. Why would her mother's best friend be calling her? Val had informed her that her mother had had a heart attack and died before she reached hospital. Annie had got the next flight home.

★　★　★

'Annie, I've found it!' came a voice from the living room as she walked in the door.

Val was kneeling on the wooden floor, holding up a very large photo album in triumph.

'I told you your mother kept some of your work,' she said.

Annie lay aside the newspaper and got down on her knees. She took the dusty album from the older woman and began to flick through, page after page of photographs she'd taken when she was a student at Cambridge and discovering her fledgling talent, all neatly pasted into the book.

'She told me she hated my work,' Annie sighed, confused, 'that I was wasting my talents with photography, that I should have studied medicine like Dad, like her before she met and married him.' Annie felt an arm around her shoulder. 'I was never good enough for her.'

'I know, I know.' Val may have been Sandra Anson's friend but she'd never been blinkered to her faults. 'But you proved her wrong, didn't you? Look at you now, making a good living. And this just goes to show that she was proud of you really, even if she didn't show it.'

It was too little, too late. Annie snapped the album shut and got up.

'Thanks for helping me sort through all this,' she said looking around the dishevelled room. There were books and papers everywhere, a mass of cushions and throws on the furniture and knick-knacks and ornaments on every surface. It was as if her mother had been trying to fill her life with stuff because she didn't have anything else.

'There's a lot to do and I know you want to get back to New York as soon as possible after the funeral.' Val smiled.

'Yes,' Annie looked out of the window. The mulberry tree was rustling in the breeze. She remembered climbing it when she was small. 'Val,' she said tentatively. 'Did you know The Priory was up for sale?'

'I had heard. Nobody seems to last long there. I wonder who will take it on next?'

Annie didn't say anything more about it. She sighed. 'Well, I'd better crack on I suppose.'

★ ★ ★

There was only so much sorting out you could do at one time. After an hour of sifting through memories Annie felt the need to get out into the fresh air. She didn't want to walk into Chattelcombe and have to face dealing with people's condolences. She wanted to be alone.

So she strode away from the village, over the stile at the end of the lane and along the path that led up over the cliffs, where she could feel the wind in her hair and hear the waves crashing on the rocks far below. One of the reasons why she loved Manhattan was because it was surrounded by water, with the Atlantic just out there in touching distance. And on the weekends there was Long Island. She needed the sea.

New York had been the perfect place to escape to. Not that she'd intended to stay, but after her assignment was over, Jessica, her colleague at the magazine, had asked her if she'd like to rent an apartment with her. As there was nothing pressing back in London, Annie had agreed. More work had come in, she'd got her Green Card, and after three years she felt settled in the Big Apple. Until now. Funny how the phone call to come home had acted like a catalyst, making her face up to the question 'Where next?'

She knew where her footsteps would lead her now; there was a secret way into the grounds — Edward had shown her all those years ago — stones removed from the wall just behind a gorse bush. Annie found it easily, but now she had to get down on her hands and knees to scramble through.

The undergrowth was wild on the other side of the wall but she knew the way. Presently tall, waxy rhododendrons parted to reveal the ruins of The Old Priory, silhouetted against a summer sky. It took the air out of her lungs. She thought she'd forgotten, buried the memories, but they were there, as real as if it were yesterday.

Next to The Priory stood the house with its ancient vine crawling up the crevices and canopying the grand entrance. The Jacobean windows winked back in the sunshine but behind the panes of glass was the blackness of an empty house. For one fleeting moment she wondered if Edward would be there, before remembering that the family were long gone. As she stood there a memory suddenly came back, searing in its focus, as if she were watching a film.

★ ★ ★

'Hello, I'm Charlotte. Do you want to play with me? You can ride my bike home after school if you like.'

Annie, standing by the shed in the school yard, playing with her plaits because she was alone and didn't want others to think she didn't have anything to do, looked up to see the new girl standing in front of her. Miss Morris had introduced her to the class that morning. She had big, dark eyes and hair curled in ringlets.

'Okay,' Annie said and after school the girl allowed her to ride the bike home while she ran alongside, twirling and dancing.

'I'm going to be a ballet dancer when I grow up,' Charlotte told her. 'I go to class in Trowminster. Madame Dubensky says I'm good enough to get into the Royal Ballet School. She's going to send me for an audition.'

'Wow!' said Annie who didn't feel she was particularly good at anything. 'Here's where I live.'

'Do you want to come and play at my

10

house?' the girl invited.

'I'll have to ask my mother. Wait for me by the gate.'

She hopped off the bike and ran inside.

'Mum, can I go and play with a new school friend? She's invited me to her house.'

Her mother was busy baking and Annie thought she might have got away with a disinterested 'yes'. Instead, her mother demanded sharply to know who the new friend was.

'Her name's Charlotte Nunce. She's just moved to the village.'

The frown on her mother's face disappeared.

'The Nunces have just moved into The Priory,' she said avariciously. Then she smiled. 'It can't harm to be friendly with them. Very well, but don't be late home.'

Annie had never been inside Chattelcombe Priory, although she'd once stolen into the grounds. The house had been empty for a while and some of the children in the village said it was haunted. She'd snuck up to it for a dare, and had run away from the brooding house and the ruins just as quickly. As she stood in the entrance hallway now she was in awe of the stained glass windows, the dark-wood panelling, the smell of beeswax and the prickly feeling that ghosts walked the corridors.

A distinguished-looking man, dressed in a baggy grey cardigan and wearing round spectacles, was crossing the hallway.

'Daddy, this is Annie,' said Charlotte.

'Hello Annie,' he said, only looking at her briefly before disappearing into one of the myriad rooms.

'Daddy's a professor,' said Charlotte. 'He does research on old languages. Come and meet Mummy.'

Mrs Nunce, as dark and pretty as her daughter, served them lemonade in the kitchen. She asked Annie lots of questions about her mother and the people in the village.

'I do hope we shall get to know people,' she said.

After a while Charlotte seemed to get bored of Annie getting all the attention. Annie enjoyed it because her own mother barely showed the slightest interest in having a conversation with her.

'Come on,' Charlotte said. 'I'll show you my ballet shoes and dresses.' Annie followed her out of the kitchen and back to the hall.

They'd reached the bottom of the stairs when a voice said, 'Who've you got there Charlie?'

Annie looked up the stairs to see a boy leaning against the banister halfway down. As a rule she didn't care for boys — they never let her join in their games and could be very cruel — but she'd never seen a boy like this one before. With dark blond hair and eyes as intense as his sister's, he looked at them arrogantly.

'Just a friend,' Charlotte said diffidently. 'This is Annie.'

'Hello Annie, I'm Edward,' said the boy.

'I'm going to show Annie my ballet things,' said Charlotte.

'Can't you think of anything more exciting than that?' he sneered. 'I'm going to explore the ruins. You can come if you like.' And with that he brushed past them.

Annie could feel the confidence oozing out of him — it made her think of that story she'd heard about the Pied Piper, mesmerising children into following him. Edward Nunce knew she wanted to follow but she'd promised Charlotte that she'd look at her tutus and shoes, even though the prospect of exploring the ruins was much more enticing. Dutifully she followed Charlotte up to her bedroom, watched as she pulled out her satin shoes and pink tutus, sipping on lemonade, her eyes darting to the window as she wondered what Edward was up to.

Charlotte must have sensed her ambivalence for, finally, she gave in.

'Do you want to go outside?' she asked tentatively, hoping the answer would be no.

'Yes, let's!'

The boy was balancing on one of the walls of the ruins, whistling quietly to himself.

'Knew you'd come,' he said, grinning at her as she sprinted up breathless in her eagerness to get there. 'Follow me.'

He took her on a tour of the ruins, exploring broken walls, nooks and crannies, rubble-strewn grass that had once been rooms, uneven steps, windows where only the crumbling honey-stoned mullions remained, Charlotte bringing up the rear.

Annie thought it was the most magical place, but perhaps that was because he was there.

'This is where they used to torture people,' he said, descending some steps to a lower level and what must once have been a boxroom. Green lichen clung to the foundation walls.

'Don't be silly. Monks didn't torture people.'

'They did if you didn't believe,' he said authoritatively. 'Sometimes when I'm in bed at night I can still hear the screams of the ghosts.'

'Stop it Edward! Stop it!' said Charlotte, covering her ears.

Annie wasn't scared. She was horribly fascinated. And even then she understood that he was a spinner of yarns.

The sun was setting in an orange haze through the skeletal west window of the chapel as, reluctantly, Annie said she had to go home.

'I will see you again soon Annie,' Edward said matter-of-factly, as if it were a given.

'Can I come and play with you again?' she asked Charlotte, trying not to sound too eager.

'Yes. You're my new friend. I like you.'

'I like you too.'

She didn't say she also liked Edward because that wasn't the sort of thing you said to boys. Besides which, she had the feeling he wouldn't care one way or the other, but she wanted to come back to The Priory again; she wanted to see Edward.

Her mother seemed pleased she'd made friends with the children at The Priory and encouraged her to visit.

From that first day Edward was always hovering in the background. Sometimes she found it annoying when she and Charlotte were caught up in a game and he was there, waiting. There were times when she wanted to do girly things, but there were also other occasions when she was ready for adventure and Edward was keen to provide it.

'Look, I'll show you a secret way in if ever the gates are locked and you want to come to visit,' he said one day.

He led her to a hole in the wall.

'I made it myself,' he said proudly. 'Just in case I need to escape quickly one day.'

She climbed through into a scrubby field where sheep grazed.

'You're not to tell anyone though,' he

warned. 'It's our secret.'

And her insides glowed at the knowledge that she shared a special secret with him.

★ ★ ★

It had been a long time ago. Annie shook herself out of the memory. Out of the corner of her eye she thought she saw something moving in the ruins. Annie squinted to see — perhaps children had found a way in, or prospective buyers were being shown around, except there were no cars on the drive or tell-tale squeals of children playing.

A cloud passed across the sun casting her in shadow and snuffing out the warmth of the day. Suddenly Annie didn't want to be there alone anymore. Quickly she turned away and beat a path back through the rhododendrons, eager to leave the past behind.

2

The vicar had arranged to call the following day to plan the service. Annie expected to see the elderly Father Jacobs who'd been in Chattelcombe forever so she was surprised to open the door to a young man with a full head of almost black hair and eyes as blue as the sky on a summer's day.

'Hello, I'm Tim Ravenwood, the vicar. You must be Annie,' he said.

'Yes,' she answered. 'Er, you'd better come in.'

She cleared a space on one of the armchairs for him.

'I'm sorry, I expected Father Jacobs,' she explained.

'He retired last year,' said the vicar. 'I'm new, I've been here eight months. Lovely parish. You're one of the old families, aren't you? Quite a few people in church have told me about your mother.'

'Oh yes?' said Annie cautiously.

'Nothing prejudicial,' he assured. 'Why don't you tell me about her so I'll know what to say in the service?'

What could Annie say? That she was an awkward woman, that she could be abrasive, that Annie had spent a lifetime fighting her disapproval and disappointment? She tried to be as fair and as non-commital as possible.

'We weren't close,' she said to finish.

'Still, she was your mother,' he smiled kindly, and for the first time Annie felt a lump in her throat. He'd found the spot no-one else had been able to.

'It's the passing of the familiar,' she said to cover it up. 'I'm next in line now that both my parents are dead.'

'Have you any other family?'

She shook her head.

'And you live abroad.'

'New York. Once I've sorted out the house after the funeral I'll be returning. Um, I'm not sure what hymns to sing at the service. My mother wasn't a great churchgoer and I haven't been much recently, sorry,' she gave an apologetic shrug.

'Not to worry,' he smiled. 'Why don't you pick a couple of these?' and he reeled off a selection of well-known, traditional hymns.

In truth, Annie had been dreading this meeting, but his relaxed manner had made it easy for her. She told him so adding, 'You're not at all like Father Jacobs.'

'I don't know whether that's a compliment or not,' he grinned.

'Oh, take it as a compliment vicar. I was dreading making these arrangement but it hasn't been as difficult as I was expecting.'

'Call me Tim.'

She shook hands with him again at the door.

'We'll try and make this a celebration of your mother's life,' he said as he turned on the doorstep. 'Don't worry about any of it.'

And then he was gone and she closed

the door again thinking what a surprise and — in a funny way, a pleasure — the encounter had been. And she was sure her mother would have appreciated having a handsome, trendy, young vicar to bury her instead of the serious-minded and often judgemental Father Jacobs.

★　★　★

Much of the village turned out for the funeral. Sandra Anson may not have been one of the most popular women in Chattelcombe but she was one of them and Chattelcombe people always looked after their own.

Tim Ravenwood led the service beautifully and after the coffin had been lowered into the ground in the churchyard where Annie's father was buried, everyone went back to the local pub for refreshments.

'Hi, do you remember me?' came a voice at Annie's shoulder.

'Teresa Finch!' Annie exclaimed. She

could hardly have forgotten the girl with the thick shock of ginger hair who played on the school hockey team with her.

'Actually it's Murdoch now,' she laughed.

'You married Dylan Murdoch, from school?'

'For my sins,' she said. 'We stuck together in the fifth form and never quite seemed to unstick again. I own the florist's shop in the village now.'

'You did the flowers for the funeral?' she asked, as Val Linton had arranged all that for her.

Teresa nodded.

'They're beautiful. You did a great job.'

'I'm sorry about your mum.'

'Thanks.'

'You should come around for a meal one evening while you're home. We can catch up on all the news.'

'That would be great.'

'Have you heard about The Priory being up for sale? Tim is hoping to buy it.'

'The vicar wants to buy The Priory?' Annie sounded surprised and cast a glance in his direction. He'd kindly consented to come to the wake and was chatting away brightly to an elderly couple in the corner of the room. He had dimples when he smiled, making him look boyish. She found herself wondering how older members of his congregation could take him seriously when he looked so young.

'The church wants to turn it into a retreat centre,' Teresa answered. 'There's a meeting about it in the village hall next Thursday. It's a colossal amount of money to raise but we'll do our best.'

A retreat centre? Well, it made sense, Annie supposed; after all it had begun life as a religious establishment. Maybe it was what the place needed after its recent history of tragedy.

Somebody else came up to talk to her then and Teresa excused herself. Gradually, as the afternoon wore on, people began to drift away.

'You go home,' Val said. 'It's been a

long day for you. I'll tidy up with a couple of friends.'

'I don't know how to thank you Val for all you've done,' Annie sighed, suddenly feeling weary.

'It's my pleasure,' she smiled. 'And it's the least I could do for Sandra. I'll come over tomorrow and help you clear out.'

It remained only to say thank you to the vicar for the service.

'It was really lovely, if you can say that about a funeral.'

'I'm delighted,' he took her hand in his warmly. His blue eyes seemed to sparkle with kindness which almost made her want to cry even though she'd managed to blink back tears all day. 'I'll call around and see you in a couple of days. Take care.'

Now the funeral was over Annie felt alone as she let herself back into the house. Strange, she never thought she'd feel like this. She made herself a cup of tea and sat down in her mother's armchair facing the empty fireplace. It was time to look forward, to what lay ahead, but ever since she'd been up to The Priory she couldn't help but look back. She allowed the memories to carry her away now.

★   ★   ★

It was Christmas and the Nunces were throwing a big party. Her mother was excited that they'd both been invited.

'Making friends with that girl was the best thing you ever did,' she said, sitting at her dressing table applying foundation as she prepared to go out.

Annie was already dressed in a lilac taffeta dress, the skirts stiffened by the layers of tulle underneath. It rustled as she moved. Her mother had taken her into town to buy it. Annie couldn't remember the last time she'd had anything new, or when her mother had last taken her anywhere.

There were Christmas lanterns strung up among the trees at The Priory, two fir trees twinkling with white lights at

26

the front door and a monstrous Christmas tree filling half the hall and reaching up to the first floor landing inside. Garlands of holly and spruce bedecked the panelling and the house seemed to smell throughout of cinnamon and spice. It was so different to her own home.

For a young girl it was a truly magical setting; but far more magical to Annie was the sight of Edward, dressed in black velvet with white ruffles at his throat.

'Don't laugh,' he frowned. 'I didn't want to wear this.'

Annie thought he looked nice and said so. Charlotte was in pink and looked like an angel.

Edward soon took charge of the other children, organising them into a game of hide and seek.

'You can come and hide with me Annie,' he said, catching her hand. Thrilled, she allowed herself to be led away by him.

'What about Charlotte?' she said, looking back. 'Can't she come and hide with us?'

'There won't be room,' he said, pulling her away and, as usual, she was overwhelmed by him.

He led her through endless rooms, finally pausing at a small cupboard door in the old nursery. They had to bend down to climb inside.

'They'll never find us in here,' he said.

He flicked a light switch to reveal shelves filled with packets of sweets and chocolate and games to play.

'This is my private collection,' he said proudly, unwrapping a bar of chocolate and offering a piece to her. 'Do you want to play a game?' He selected a board-game from the shelf and they sat down on the floor to play it together.

Annie could have stayed there forever with him, but Edward quickly became bored.

'I want to get back to the party,' he yawned. 'People will wonder where we've been hiding.'

He always liked to be the centre of attention and he always got his own way. Annie suspected that the reason they got on so well together was that she never questioned him.

'Don't tell anyone else about this secret place,' he said as they climbed out again. 'You know about it because you're special.'

She smiled. Back at the party everyone gathered around him but that didn't matter. She knew she was special and that no-one could break into that tight cocoon they'd spun around themselves.

But the night had ended on a discordant note. She remembered her mother who'd had too much to drink and was in the corner of the drawing room making inappropriate gestures towards the professor. She remembered Edward chuckling at the spectacle while all she could do was feel mortified at the sight of Mr Naylor, the local solicitor and Father Jacobs trying to rescue the poor man from her mother's tipsy overtures.

★ ★ ★

Annie snapped back to reality. There were so many things she'd tried to bury, but each in turn seemed to be resurfacing.

That's what funerals did, she supposed; made you face the past before you could move on to the future.

Tim Ravenwood was as good as his word and called back to see her a couple of days later.

'How are you coping?' he asked, declining the cup of tea she offered.

'Getting on with it,' she shrugged in reply. 'Clearing the house is going to be a huge task. Then I'll have to put it up for sale. Teresa Murdoch was telling me at the funeral that you're thinking of buying The Priory.'

'Are you familiar with it?'

'I spent quite a bit of my childhood there. I was friendly with the Nunces.'

'It would make a great retreat centre,' he said. 'Unfortunately we're not the only interested party and it's going to be very expensive. There's a meeting on Thursday in the village hall to try and

30

put something together.'

'I might be interested in coming to that,' Annie found herself saying. 'I'm at a bit of a loose end here really.'

'We'd love your support,' he enthused. 'Particularly as you have a connection with the place.'

'I'll be there then,' she promised.

★ ★ ★

On Thursday Annie turned up at the village hall.

'Hi Annie, come and sit with us,' Teresa Murdoch waved from across the room. Annie slipped into the empty chair at her side and Teresa patted her leg in sympathy before turning her attention to the front as Tim stood up.

'I've called this meeting so that we can devise a strategy for purchasing The Priory,' he began. 'I think it would make an ideal retreat centre. I know it has a reputation, some of you have told me about the tragedies that have occurred there over the years, but surely it's time to redeem the place, to return it to its religious foundations.'

It sounded like sound reasoning to Annie.

'Now, it's going to be difficult to raise the money,' he continued. 'The Diocese are prepared to put in some, but we will need to find the remainder of it ourselves.'

'Plenty of fundraising events then, vicar,' said a man at the front.

'I think we'll need more than that, Bill. We'll have to have a gift day for a start; it's time for us all to start making big pledges if we're to pull this off. Don't forget, we're not the only interested party.'

Annie looked around as the discussion continued. She saw commitment on people's faces, passion for a vision; they seemed prepared to follow Tim Ravenwood which was no mean feat in this village. She liked his manner, he didn't try to steamroller people and he listened to everyone's opinion, however outrageous, and took it on board.

'How's your new vicar working out?' she asked Teresa casually as the meeting came to a close with the formation of a committee and a number of ideas to pursue.

'He's great,' she enthused. 'Remember old Father Jacobs?'

'How could I forget? So dour, reminding us that we were all going to burn in hell.'

'Yes, I remember that was the last school assembly he was allowed to do,' Teresa chuckled. 'I wasn't really a church-goer until Tim turned up. Do you know he's visited every house in the village?'

Annie followed Teresa's fond gaze to the stage where his dark head was almost lost in a sea of heads bowed together in discussion.

'He's already done a lot of good for the church in this parish. Whatever he came up with, I think I'd support him one hundred per cent.'

'Is he married?' Annie asked.

'No, why?' Teresa looked at her keenly.

Annie laughed.

'I didn't mean it in that way,' she said. 'It's just that he seems like a really nice chap, really decent. You expect someone like that to be married.'

'We could do with a few more like him,' Teresa sighed. 'Anyway, what about that meal? Do you want to come around tomorrow?'

Annie answered absently for her mind was suddenly on Edward again. In no way could he have been described as decent or really nice. Edward had been exciting and glamorous — he also had had a dangerous edge. But Edward had been a long time ago and she'd tried to forget him.

★   ★   ★

Teresa lived with her husband and young son at the other end of the village in a new build with perfect lawns and a caravan in the driveway.

Annie wasn't the only guest who'd been invited that evening; as she entered the dining room the vicar was already seated at the table.

'I asked Tim to come too,' Teresa explained. 'You know what bachelors are like, don't feed themselves properly.'

'Teresa is the best cook in the parish,' Tim flattered and she blushed with pleasure.

Annie wasn't sure what to think of this unexpected situation. Was Teresa matchmaking after what she'd said at the meeting yesterday?

'Annie, why don't you sit here?' Teresa indicated the chair on the left-hand side of the vicar. Tim rose quickly to pull it out for her, smiling warmly as he did so.

'Thanks,' she said.

He wasn't wearing his collar tonight, just jeans and an open-necked cotton shirt, the blue check picking out the colour of his eyes. Remarkable eyes, she thought, before quickly looking away and holding out her glass as Dylan offered wine.

'Nice house,' she said.

'I bet you've got a trendy loft apartment in Manhattan,' Teresa said as she started serving the home-made lasagne.

'Not quite. I'm a freelance photographer so although there are times when I'm doing well, there are plenty of lean times too. I rent with a flatmate; I couldn't afford anything else.'

'Male or female?' Teresa asked.

'That's a subtle question,' Dylan rolled his eyes.

'Well, I'm nosy,' Teresa laughed.

'I was seeing someone until about six months ago,' Annie said, conscious of Tim at her side. 'Benton was a freelance photographer too, but we were apart so much. He did a lot of location work, so we decided to end it. It was never serious, just convenient.' None of her relationships had lasted long and she had a theory as to why that should be.

'It must be an exciting life,' Teresa sighed, fork paused halfway to her mouth. 'Dylan and I have stayed in

Chattelcombe and, as you can see from the caravan, we tend to take our holidays in this country, when we can get away from the business that is.'

'We're quite boring really,' Dylan winked.

Annie remembered him as being solid and dependable in school, not one of the boys who shone at sports or academic work, or who was particularly popular with the girls. She'd always felt sorry for Teresa because she had charismatic Edward, and who could compare with him? But maybe Teresa was the lucky one after all, for she and Dylan seemed well-matched and happy and immensely proud of four-year-old Alan.

'I don't remember you studying photography,' Teresa frowned. 'Didn't you do medicine at Cambridge?'

'Biochemistry. I changed my mind, dropped out and turned my hobby into a profession.'

There were other reasons why she'd left Cambridge which she didn't want to go into now.

'I admire people who do that,' Tim suddenly spoke up at her side.

'What, drop out?'

'Turn hobbies into professions.'

'I thought you had a vocation. Isn't that sort of similar?'

'I guess it is.'

'Tim keeps telling us he was strong-armed into the ministry.' Teresa laughed as she looked at him.

Annie looked surprised.

'Not literally, don't worry,' he offered her more salad, holding the bowl while she spooned lettuce onto her plate. 'I always say 'the man upstairs' got me.'

'What did you do before?' Annie asked.

'Travelled, made music, taught, did care work. Then people started telling me what I should be doing. I figured it was God speaking.'

'And you were made for this work,' Teresa enthused.

'I was in an inner city parish before coming here,' he nodded in acknowlegement. 'So Chattelcombe is quite a contrast.'

'Oh, we have our secrets,' Teresa said ominously.

That was a little too close for comfort for Annie. But her instincts about Tim Ravenwood had been confirmed — he really wasn't a traditional vicar. And he was easy to talk to. She didn't have to be on her best behaviour at all and found herself relaxing into the convivial warmth of the evening, forgetting about her mother, the house and The Priory.

Over coffee Teresa said, 'Now The Priory's up for sale, it's got me thinking,' she smoothed the cat curled up on her lap. 'Do you ever hear from Edward Nunce? You and he were thick as thieves when you were growing up.'

'No,' Annie said quickly. 'It was a long time ago. We lost touch.'

The emphatic denial made Tim study her keenly, as if he knew there was more to it.

'Sad what happened to Charlotte,' Teresa sighed.

'I try not to think about it.'

'Talking about The Priory,' Tim

changed the subject — it was subtle but Annie picked up on it and was grateful. 'We're going to look at it tomorrow — the church council. We've got an appointment with the estate agent.'

'I think you're all mad,' Dylan grunted.

'Can I come?' the words were out before Annie'd even had a chance to think about it. 'I mean, it's years since I've been inside. I'd like to, for old times' sake.'

'We'd be delighted to have you,' Tim smiled.

Eventually Annie said she ought to be getting home, although she had nothing to go back to.

'I'll walk with you,' Tim got up too. 'The vicarage is on the way.'

Teresa winked at her by the door as she said goodnight.

'Don't go getting any ideas,' Annie hissed.

The sun had gone down and the night was perfumed with the scent of cut grass.

'So, did you spend your whole

childhood in Chattelcombe,' Tim asked as they walked slowly side by side along the main street leading back into the village.

'Yes, and got away as soon as I could.'

'To Cambridge?'

'Yes. Did you go to university?'

'London,' he said. 'I come from a small mining community in Nottinghamshire. I had to get out and see the big, wide world. You can't do an awful lot with an English degree, except teach, so I did — EFL out in Thailand and then South America, just for a couple of years. You know what I discovered?'

She looked at him.

'The landscape changes but people don't.'

'I thought your faith was all about changing people?'

'My faith?' he challenged. 'It's not yours anymore?'

She shrugged. 'I don't know.'

'Yeah, people can change.' He smiled.

41

'If I didn't think that I wouldn't be in this job. They've got to want to though.'

She was thinking of Edward again; thinking of him even with this very attractive and unconventional vicar walking at her side.

'What I meant is that people are the same wherever you go,' he explained. 'You've got to pick a group to work with and stick with them.'

'I wonder if that's why I enjoy freelancing?' Annie speculated. 'I don't have to work with any particular group. I'm just me, a free agent.' She deliberately brushed the image of Edward aside.

'Sooner or later you'll have to settle for something, belong somewhere,' Tim warned. 'That's where the joy comes from.'

She stopped walking and looked into his blue eyes.

'No, you really are nothing like Father Jacobs at all!'

He laughed, an infectious, life-affirming laugh that lit up his face and made her want to join in.

'The vicarage,' she said when they reached the big house on the corner. 'I think I can reach my home safely from here — having survived riding the New York subway I think Chattelcombe High Street will be a doddle.'

He grinned.

'See you tomorrow,' he said. 'Eleven o'clock.'

'I'll see you there.'

3

Annie reflected on the evening, particularly Teresa's comment: 'Sad what happened to Charlotte.' Annie could say she tried not to think about it as much as she liked, when in reality it seemed to occupy an awful lot of her thoughts these days. And now, with the prospect of seeing inside the house again tomorrow, she could think of nothing else.

Sleep would not come. She sat up against the pillows listening to the whisperings of the night and let the past sweep over her once again.

She remembered the day — it was a glorious summer morning, a week before Charlotte's audition for the Royal Ballet School. She and Edward had been playing a board-game on the floor of the library when Charlotte had appeared. She'd been to have her hair cut and skipped into the room feeling pleased with her short bob.

'Can I play?' she'd asked.

'We're in the middle of a game,' Edward had said curtly.

Charlotte had sat cross-legged on the floor anyway. Edward had flicked a signal with his eyes at Annie and in the next moment they'd jumped up together and sprinted from the room, leaving a protesting Charlotte behind.

'Wait for me! Why do you always run away from me?'

Annie felt sorry for her, but Edward's energy lured her on.

'Come on Annie, run!' He laughed as he sped out of the kitchen door and through the pottager, almost bowling into Henry Mace, the gardener.

'Where are we going?' she called out breathlessly.

He led her to the ruins.

'She'll easily find us in here,' Annie bent over double, hands on knees as she tried to catch her breath.

'Yeah, but we can lead her all over

the place. That'll make her cry.'

Annie didn't particularly want to make Charlotte cry.

'What's the matter Charlie?' Edward taunted as she approached. He jumped up onto a wall.

'You're so bad Edward!' Charlotte accused.

'Come on then, if you want to join us.'

As soon as she began running towards them, Edward jumped down and caught Annie's hand.

'Run!' He laughed.

'Edward, wait!' shouted Charlotte.

They dodged in and out of the ruins, always one step ahead of Charlotte who grew increasingly frustrated. If it had been her, Annie would have stopped playing Edward's game ages ago.

Finally, even Charlotte grew tired.

'I don't care anymore,' she cried out from halfway down some uneven steps. 'I'm going to tell Daddy what you're doing. I'll tell him what you did to my dolls and my new dress, and I'll tell him what you said to . . . '

'Oh no you won't,' Edward clambered up the side of the wall so that he was above her on the steps.

That was one threat that would work on Edward. Annie had seen how the professor had a soft spot for his daughter, while with Edward there was an absence of warmth.

'Yes I will!' Charlotte threatened again in a rare moment of strength.

It was all over in a moment: the push from Edward, Charlotte stepping back then losing her footing, her scream as she fell and the thud as she hit the hard ground, her limbs splayed at impossible angles.

'Edward!' Annie screamed.

Charlotte began to whimper like a wounded animal.

'It was an accident,' he said, his face suddenly white. 'She tripped.'

'You pushed her.'

'She shouldn't have threatened me.'

'We'd better get someone.'

He hesitated.

'Daddy, Daddy,' Charlotte moaned, while he stood looking at her.

'Edward!' Annie cried again.

'It was an accident,' he said, looking at her now, willing her to agree. 'You're my secret keeper Annie. Promise me!'

'An accident,' she'd nodded. 'I won't tell.'

Only then did he set off at a sprint for the house, as if a light had suddenly come on in his head. It was an accident; he hadn't intended to do anything more than scare her, or maybe hurt her, but not this, never this. Annie felt terrified of being left alone with the twitching Charlotte.

'Don't worry Charlotte,' she sat at her side and tried to soothe her. 'It'll be alright. Edward's gone for help.'

'Daddy,' the cry was fading.

After what seemed like forever Mrs Nunce appeared, wailing as she saw her daughter.

'Don't move her ma'am,' the housekeeper advised.

The image of a mother wanting to

cradle her child and being unable to was seared on Annie's memory. She remembered the siren of the ambulance, watched from a distance as they took Charlotte away. Only when it was over did she retch into the sun-burned grass. Edward was nowhere to be seen.

She heard later that Charlotte's cries for her father went unanswered. No-one knew where the professor was, and by the time he eventually came home and discovered what had happened, Charlotte had been operated on and was in a coma for the next couple of days. She was in hospital and rehabilitation afterwards and, when she did return home, all hopes of an audition were gone. In fact, it soon became clear that her hopes of ever becoming a ballet dancer were gone, too. Shattered bones mended but Charlotte didn't.

'I'm sorry Charlotte,' Annie had said when she visited.

'You let him do it,' Charlotte accused. 'You were always on Edward's side, never mine. Go away!'

Like Charlotte, the friendship was broken.

★ ★ ★

Annie felt apprehensive as she drove up to Chattelcombe Priory the following morning. Was the child who'd played here all those years ago still in her? Would Edward seem real? Would it still hurt as much? Or perhaps she'd finally be able to lay some ghosts to rest.

The gates stood open revealing the drive lined with horse chestnuts powdering pollen along the gravel. From this aspect the house looked welcoming, the ruins of The Priory alongside, obscured by the spreading branches of an ancient spruce. As she swung past it she glanced across and, for a brief moment, could have sworn she saw a figure flitting past a gap in the chapel wall. It was impossible! The mind was playing tricks! She squeezed her eyes shut for a second before looking ahead to where a line of cars were pulled up in front of the house. A group of people were gathered together on the steps.

Teresa waved as Annie got out of the car. Tim beamed a smile at her.

'I've always wanted to see inside this place,' Teresa confided. 'You know I used to be quite jealous of you playing up at the big house. You never invited me to come with you.'

No, because she'd never wanted to share Edward with anyone.

'Well now's your chance,' Annie smiled weakly.

The estate agent led them inside. A wave of nostalgia swept over Annie as she stood in the hallway once more, smelling the familiar smell, watching dust dancing in shafts of sunlight. The wood panelling seemed darker than she remembered, perhaps because there were no family portraits and paintings to break up the unrelenting black. The carpet on the stairs appeared worn. Everything had a faint patina of neglect about it. The surprising thing was that she felt an ache, a longing for what had been lost, mingled with that old frisson of fear, of unpredictability.

She looked towards the grand staircase. That's where she'd first seen Edward looking confident and arrogant as he leaned against the banister, knowing that she'd find him far more interesting than his sister. She felt a stab of pain at the memory now and sadness for that poor, gullible girl who'd wasted years on unfulfilled expectations.

★　★　★

Edward had arranged to meet her outside the church of Great St. Mary.

'There's something I want to tell you!' he'd sounded full of excitement on the phone. 'I meant to tell you yesterday but, well, wait and see.'

Yesterday they'd sat by the river enjoying a picnic in the early spring weather, books spread out under a willow tree as they studied together.

Punts had glided by on the Cam and all had seemed well with the world. It was how she had dreamed it would be.

Annie had expected to see more of Edward when she'd come up to Cambridge too, but their paths didn't cross as much as she'd hoped. They were in different colleges and he had a separate group of friends. Besides which, life was hectic with lectures and practicals and studying in the library. To spend a whole day together had been like heaven. It reminded her of their childhood years when he'd been exclusively hers.

She waited for Edward now, feeling rising anticipation, watching early season tourists clicking away with their cameras pointed at King's College Chapel. Cyclists whizzed by and a lone blackbird sang noisily from a bush in the churchyard.

Then she saw him, hurrying towards her through the crowds, the first glimpse of him always with the power to thrill — that smile, blond hair flopping into his eyes, college scarf flying about him — surely the most handsome man in the whole university and certainly the most interesting.

'Hi Annie,' he kissed her on the cheek and she savoured the smell of his spicy aftershave.

'So, what's this great news?' she couldn't mask the hope in her voice. She'd always hoped and waited for the right time. 'It had better be good because I'm missing a lecture.'

'It's better than good,' he grinned. 'I wanted you to be the first to know: I've just got engaged!'

She opened her mouth to speak but nothing came out. In fact, she could barely breathe, stunned with the revelation. In that instant her world came crashing down about her.

Edward, being Edward, chose to ignore her reaction and carried on talking eagerly.

'Her name's Natasha,' he said. 'She's studying modern languages. Her parents live in Switzerland. Her dad's a diplomat. Oh God, Annie, she's the most beautiful girl!'

'How long have you been seeing her?' Annie found her voice although it was a croak.

'Since halfway through Michaelmas term.'

Months and months! And no mention of it! No hint that he was with someone. Not even at Christmas when they'd been home, when they'd danced together at the party and kissed under the mistletoe!

'She's over there, waiting in the coffee shop,' he pointed. 'Do you want to come and meet her?'

That was too much.

'No,' she said breathlessly. 'Edward!'

The protest in her voice got his full attention.

'You know how I feel about you. I thought, from that first day at The Priory, I've always believed that you and me . . . That you were waiting for the right moment.'

'Come on Annie, we were children,'

he flashed her that charming smile.

'I'm your secret keeper!'

'And you'll always keep them, I know,' he clasped her hand between his and leaned close. 'We're friends. It was never more than that. You're my best friend. Be happy for me.'

Yarn spinner, enticer, like the Pied Piper. She knew what he was, yet she'd allowed herself to be drawn in, thinking that she was different, believing that she was immune, that he was exclusively hers, that they belonged together. How wrong she'd been. She'd allowed herself to be led because she'd wanted to be his acolyte. It was the two of them against the world. But in the end he'd chosen someone else over her.

'So are you coming to meet her?' he let go of her hand, shuffling his feet on the ground impatiently.

'How can you spring this on me and expect me to accept it just like that?' she cried, distraught.

'I'd be happy for you,' he accused. He shoved his hands deep into his pockets and shrugged. 'Look Annie, I can't keep her waiting. Are you coming or not?'

She shook her head.

'Then I'm sorry. I've got to go. I'll see you around.'

Except he didn't. After that he never rang her, never sought her out. Once or twice she saw him about the town, hand in hand with a beautiful blonde girl; once she'd seen them kissing and had had to do a detour to get away from the gut-wrenching sight. In the long summer holiday she stayed away from Chattelcombe Priory only to discover that he hadn't even bothered coming home.

'Perhaps you didn't give him what he wanted,' her mother taunted her. 'He was yours for the taking after all.'

But Annie didn't know what else she could have done and it took a long while for her heart to mend. She deliberately blocked out everything to do with his engagement and wedding. The old life was dead. She left

Cambridge, abandoned her studies, picked up her camera and moved to London with her mother's condemnation ringing in her ears. She had to discover who the real Annie Anson was, without him.

★ ★ ★

She still didn't know after all these years.

'Are you okay?' Teresa said at her side.

'Yeah,' she shook herself. 'Just remembering things.'

'We'd better catch up with everyone else.'

Only then did Annie realise that the rest of the party had moved on leaving her standing alone, gazing at the staircase of memories.

As she followed from room to room Annie barely heard the sales patter of the estate agent. She didn't need to; she knew every nook and cranny of this house, all the places she and Edward had explored and hidden in. She wondered if he'd point out the cubby hole in the nursery, but he seemed unaware of it. Annie held back after the group had moved through and quickly opened the door. Inside was empty, the shelves devoid of games and chocolate bars. What had she expected? The dust was thick on the shelves and on the floor saying that it hadn't been used for some time.

'Of course, when the current owners bought the house from the Nunce family,' the commentary was running as she caught up with the group once again, 'they intended to live here permanently, but other commitments have meant they were only in residence infrequently and the house has stood empty for the past eighteen months. As a consequence it does need a little bit of attention.'

'Not as much as The Priory next door,' somebody quipped.

'I heard it was haunted,' came another comment.

The agent — a young man with a flash suit and slicked-back hair — looked perturbed, not sure whether its reputation was a selling point or not, and Annie thought of the figure she thought she'd seen as she arrived.

'Well, that's why we're here,' Tim said confidently. 'To lay those ghosts to rest.'

'What happened to the Nunces anyway?' that was the man named Bill who'd spoken at the meeting the other evening.

'After they split up I think the wife and daughter emigrated to Australia,' Teresa answered. 'And didn't the professor die soon afterwards?'

Nobody seemed able to elaborate and Annie made sure she was tucked away at the back of the group so that nobody would think to ask her. What did she know? It had been so long ago.

They moved on.

'Is it as you remember?' Tim sidled up to her as they gathered in the large dining room with two ugly chandeliers suspended from ceiling roses and a view over the front lawns.

'Pretty much,' she said.

'Must have been a great place for kids. Loads of places to get lost in.'

If only he knew how true that was.

'I can already see how we can use this place,' he enthused. 'There's bags of room.'

'Have you had any other interested parties?' Teresa suddenly asked the estate agent.

'Yes,' he answered. 'This property has attracted a lot of interest. We've already had a couple of viewings and I have another scheduled for the day after tomorrow.'

There were mutterings of disappointment.

'If it's the right thing, it'll be ours,' Tim advised them all and that seemed to lift the mood.

Wishful thinking, Annie mused. Just because you really wanted something and thought it would be good didn't mean that it was going to happen. Life wasn't like that. And she didn't know if

God could fix things either. What if you really prayed for one thing and an equally good person prayed for the exact opposite? Which one was God going to say 'yes' to? It was a very imprecise way of doing things. The vicar seemed to believe it though, judging by the look of conviction on his face. If only she could have the same certainties.

The tour over they came back to the hallway, the estate agent summing up his presentation. He ceased mid flow and suddenly changed tack as he looked towards the front door.

'I'm sorry, I wasn't expecting you today.'

'That's all right. I was in the area. I thought I'd drive up and then I could see there was a party here and the door was open,' came a man's smooth, confident voice. Annie recognised it instantly, even though she hadn't heard it for so many years and her heart skipped a beat. 'Well I hope you're ready to put in an incredible offer ladies and gentlemen. You'll need to, because I'm the competition.'

Annie stepped out from behind the church group and stifled a gasp as she recognised the figure standing in the doorway — it was Edward Nunce. Edward saw her at the same time and the self-assured look slipped from his face. For a long moment they stared, each as shocked as the other. He was just as she remembered him — golden beauty, intense eyes, arrogant mouth, effortless style — except the floppy fringe was gone and his hair was beginning to recede; it made him look distinguished.

He was the last person she would have expected to see here, and because the association was too raw, too painful, she gave her apologies to Tim and pushed past Edward into the open air where she could breathe more easily. She thought she heard him whisper her name as she rushed past him.

Annie slammed the car door, fumbled with her keys in the ignition and then drove away, hands shaking on the wheel. Not once did she look back through her rearview mirror. She needed to put as much distance between herself and Edward Nunce as she could.

4

At home again, Annie slammed the front door — as if that could shut him out — and perched on the edge of the green sofa surrounded by boxes in the sitting room, wondering if he would follow her. But that was not Edward's style; he'd never been a follower.

Her heart was still racing. How could he still have this effect on her after all these years, after all he'd done? She wasn't a child anymore: she'd moved on, she had a career, she didn't need him.

Annie looked around the dishevelled room, half the things still unpacked and wondered why her mother had had to die now, at this particular moment when The Priory was up for sale and Edward had returned. She didn't really believe in fate, was doubtful about Tim Ravenwood's God. Even so, this was a remarkable coincidence. Perhaps her mother was having her revenge, she thought wryly.

After a while, when she was certain Edward wouldn't come, she began to relax, pottering around the house and among her mother's things in an attempt to distract herself.

The sound of the door knocker made her snap to attention.

All of her senses were on edge again as she went to answer it. Tim stood on the doorstep.

'May I come in?' he asked.

She took him into the kitchen where she made a pot of tea and shook some chocolate biscuits from a half-eaten packet onto a garish china plate.

'You disappeared rather quickly. I wondered if everything was alright?' Tim perched on one of the stools at the table and dunked a biscuit into his tea. When she didn't answer immediately he continued, 'I'm guessing you and Edward Nunce had something together. When Teresa said last night that you and he used to be as thick as thieves when you were kids . . . sometimes these things develop.'

She looked at him sharply, amazed at his insight. Although Annie barely knew him, she felt she could trust him; he had a manner which encouraged confidences which was one of the attributes that made him a good vicar, she supposed.

'I always assumed we'd end up together,' she traced the rim of her cup with her index finger. 'We were always together as children and teenagers. We both went to Cambridge to study.' She took a deep breath. 'He let me down badly there, got engaged to someone else totally out of the blue,' she looked up at Tim. His startling eyes registered understanding. 'I heard they got married, but then I lost touch and decided to get on with my own life. I went to London and then abroad and rarely came home. And when I did I never went near The Priory. Then I heard the family had sold up.' She picked up her cup in two hands. 'I just didn't expect to see him today.'

'Bit of a shock,' Tim nodded.

She didn't mention anything about their complex past.

'I'll get over it,' she offered a wry smile before sipping her tea. 'So, he wants to buy The Priory,' she said, shifting the focus.

'And he can,' Tim looked worried. 'He'll probably put in a better offer than ours. I'll just have to persuade the vendors that we'll do the old place more justice.'

'Well, anything I can do to help.'

'Thank you.' He smiled.

He didn't pursue the Edward thing any further but finished his tea and chocolate biscuit and then said that he had some parish visiting to be getting on with.

'You're sure you're all right?' he paused at the front door.

'I'll be fine,' she assured him.

She watched him go down the garden path and didn't shut the door until he had driven away. She was pondering upon how kind it was of him to check on her when she could hardly be called a member of his flock when the phone rang.

'Annie, it's Teresa. Look, I couldn't call on you, I had to get back to the shop. Are you okay? I couldn't believe it when Edward Nunce appeared. You went as white as a sheet.'

'I'm fine. Don't worry about it. It was a bit of a shock but I'm over it now. The vicar's just called.'

'Oh has he?' Teresa said knowingly.

Despite herself Annie chuckled.

'It's nothing like that.'

'Hmm. We'll have to get you two together again,' Teresa said.

'Don't bother. I won't be around for long. I've got a life to get back to.'

'Just don't let Edward Nunce distract you.'

She certainly had no intention of allowing that to happen!

And yet, when she went out to shop later that day she almost expected to bump into him in the village. How strange she must have appeared to people, peering around shop doors before entering, darting furtive glances across the street.

She was just congratulating herself on getting back home after an Edward-free shopping trip when the phone rang. Quickly she dumped the bags on the table and went into the hallway to answer it.

'Hello, Annie Anson,' she announced breezily.

'Annie, it's Edward.'

For a moment she couldn't speak.

'Annie, are you there?'

'Yes. How did you get my number?' Her mother, a very private person, had been ex-directory.

'You think I've forgotten it after all this time?' he chided. 'It was good to see you today. A bit of a shock but, yes, good. I didn't know you were back in Chattelcombe.'

'My mother died,' she said without expression, still reeling from the sound of his voice.

'Oh, I didn't know. I'm sorry. Although she was a difficult shrew and did you no favours.' There it was: that biting honesty wrapped up in a voice as smooth as toffee. 'Listen, I'd love to meet up while I'm here,' he continued. 'Do you think we might?'

'Er . . . ' her mind was all over the place.

'I'm staying at The George Hotel in Trowminster. Why don't you meet me there for dinner tonight? We can catch up for old times' sake.'

'Are you alone?' she found herself asking.

'Quite alone.'

She heard the smile in his voice. He knew he had her. Why not? For old times' sake. Just to see what he was like now.

'Okay,' she agreed. 'I'll meet you for dinner.'

'Seven o'clock?' he suggested.

'I'll be there.'

'I can hardly wait. It'll be great to catch up.'

But as she replaced the receiver Annie wondered what she'd done.

★ ★ ★

She had nothing to wear, nothing dressy at any rate. Maybe that was a good thing; she wasn't going to make an effort for Edward Nunce, it was just dinner. In the end she pulled out the black dress she'd worn to her mother's funeral, along with the black jacket and shoes. Now she looked as if she were going to another funeral. Nevertheless she applied some make-up and washed, dried and styled her long, auburn hair; it had always been difficult to tame and she usually tied it back in a knot, but tonight she let it cascade past her shoulders.

The George was Trowminster's only five star hotel and restaurant. She could remember as a child wondering what it would be like to dine there. Well, now she was about to find out.

Her heart was thumping as she

parked the car and made her way to the restaurant entrance. Laughter and conversation drifted across from the bar terrace in the evening sunshine.

'May I help you?' the Maitre d' asked her.

'Yes, I'm meeting Edward Nunce. He's a guest here.'

'Ah yes, Mr Nunce is waiting — table six in the corner.'

Edward rose immediately as she entered the restaurant so she didn't have to search for the table. Although it was still light outside lamps were lit in the low-beamed, dark-panelled room.

'Annie,' he greeted her with a smile. 'I'm glad you came.'

She shied away as he leaned over to kiss her cheek.

'Let me take your jacket,' he said, not missing a beat, and then he held the chair out for her to sit down. 'All in black,' he commented. 'Expecting it to be that bad?'

'It was my mother's funeral,' she said coolly.

'Oh, I forgot.'

'I came home from New York for it. I travelled light. I wasn't anticipating being wined and dined.'

He clicked his fingers for the waiter then sat down opposite her.

'What do you want to drink? If I remember rightly it's a dry white wine.'

It still was. He delivered the order. Annie picked up the menu, not wanting to look at him; it stirred up too many conflicting feelings.

'So Annie, how have you been?' he began. 'New York eh?'

'I'm a freelance photographer.'

'I thought you were going to be a doctor?'

'My plans changed,' she looked at him coolly over the top of the menu.

'Lots of plans changed in those days,' he acknowledged.

She ordered the most expensive starter she could see on the menu. 'I presume you're paying.'

He smiled, that lop-sided smile she remembered so well, entertained by her bolshiness. He was still beautiful, still had the power to captivate and she berated herself for feeling it.

'So,' she said as they waited. 'How's your wife?'

He chuckled.

'I can't blame you for asking, get the difficult stuff out of the way at the beginning,' he sat back as the waiter opened a napkin and spread it on his lap. 'We split up a year after the wedding.'

'Did you move on to someone else?' Annie asked tartly.

'Actually it was Natasha that left me. I didn't want to have any kids,' he shrugged it off.

Did he want her to feel sorry for him? She felt anything but. If he'd experienced one tenth of the pain she had at being rejected then there was some justice in the world.

'What about you, are you with anyone?'

'None of your business.'

'Touché!' He smiled.

The food arrived.

'So, that group you were with earlier today, I didn't take you for a church-goer,' he said.

'I'm not.'

'You haven't been confessing any-thing lately have you?' His eyes locked into hers.

'I'm your secret keeper,' she reminded him. 'I haven't said a word. Tim, the vicar, did my mother's funeral. The church wants to buy The Priory and turn it into a retreat centre.'

'Really?' She could tell he was trying not to laugh.

'Why do you want to buy it?' she challenged.

'It's good land for development,' he answered practically. 'I want to build a golf course and some houses and turn the house into a luxury hotel. I'd demolish it if it wasn't listed . . . '

'Don't you sense the ghosts?' she said urgently, lowering her voice.

This time he did laugh.

'Come on Annie, get a grip. Life

moves on. Lay your ghosts to rest.'

Her ghosts? They were his. He was the same old Edward, ready to move on, never accountable.

'I still think about those days, about Charlotte. Especially now I'm back in Chattelcombe. How is Charlotte? She's never answered any of my letters.'

'Charlotte died last year in a car accident.'

'What!' Annie felt as if all the air was being squeezed out of her.

'She was on her way to work at school, a car shot out of a junction right across her path,' he shrugged. 'Nothing anyone could do.'

'Poor Charlotte, poor Charlotte.' Annie shook her head. 'I'm sorry I could never make things right.'

'Listen, Charlie was never going to let go of the past,' Edward counselled clinically. 'Nobody could have put things right.'

'Don't you feel just a little bit guilty?'

'What's the point? It's in the past.'

'I hope you don't get The Priory!'

Annie suddenly said vehemently. 'You don't deserve it.'

'It was my home,' he said. 'I think I deserve it more than your church group on that basis alone.' Then he sighed and picked up his wine glass. 'I don't want to argue Annie. I want to catch up. I want it to be like old times. We were best friends.'

'As you say, life moves on.'

There was tension in the air as they continued their meal. As she seemed loath to speak anymore, he chatted away, telling her about his various business interests, how he'd started off in banking after getting his degree, investing his annual bonuses wisely and was now in a position to put in an offer for Chattelcombe Priory to develop it.

'I lived in Geneva for a couple of years,' he told her. 'Tash and I had a base there and I liked it, so I stayed on after the divorce. The last few years I've been back in London. Plus I've got an apartment in Venice, just off the Grand Canal. Have you ever been to Venice?'

'Twice actually, once on holiday, once for work.'

'You should come and stay with me,' he smiled.

She arched an eyebrow. It was hard to keep up this indifference with him sitting across the table from her — the smell of his aftershave, the contrast of a white shirt collar against the darkness of his skin, the capable hands with the scar across the base of his index finger where he'd once torn it on barbed wire when they were both scrabbling under a fence.

He must have noticed her looking at it for he raised his right hand and inspected the scar himself.

'Yeah, I remember,' he nodded. 'We had some great times, Annie, didn't we?'

She didn't respond.

The waiter reappeared. 'Dessert?'

'No,' she said quickly. She didn't want to stay any longer than was necessary.

'Just bring coffee,' Edward signalled.

'Ah, Annie,' he sighed and looked at her intently. 'Sometimes, when I look back to Cambridge I think — did we make a mistake all those years ago?'

' 'We' had nothing to do with it! It was your decision!' she said, anger flaring.

'Perhaps fate has presented us with another chance, an opportunity to do what we should have done then. Maybe it's not a coincidence that we've met up in this place at this time.'

'You're assuming a lot.' Her fingers playing upon the stem of her wine glass gave away her agitation and she forced herself to stop. 'Thanks for the offer but I have a life now.' Annie turned in her chair and fumbled for her bag. 'I think I'd better go. Thanks for the meal. It was good to catch up.'

As she rose from her chair he did too and caught her by the wrist.

'Annie, wait.' He must have felt her pulse racing as his thumb rubbed her wrist. 'Look, I'm sorry. I know how you felt . . .'

'You always enjoyed playing games, Edward,' she accused him, sadly.

'Can I see you again? I'm around for the next few days. Just for old times' sake?'

She managed to slip out of his grasp and shrugged on her jacket.

'I don't think it's a good idea.'

'I'll call you,' he smiled. There it was again: the assumption that he could do what Edward did best — charm and get his own way.

Annie wished him goodnight. As she walked away she knew he was watching her; she could feel that invisible connection she'd thought had been irrevocably severed that early spring day outside the church of Great St Mary in Cambridge.

★   ★   ★

It was time she put the house on the market, even though it was nowhere near ready for sale. The following afternoon Annie drove into Trowminster again, deliberately not looking at

The George Hotel as she passed it, and called in at Black and Peterson's, the estate agents.

'Hi, I'm Paul, how may I help you?' said a young man wearing a sharp suit and looking as if he was barely out of school.

She slipped into the chair before his desk. 'I want to put my house in Chattelcombe on the market.'

She spent half an hour giving him the details and making arrangements for a valuation. As she was getting up to leave the door opened and Tim Ravenwood appeared.

'Hello,' his face lit up when he saw her.

'Hi,' she smiled.

'Sorting out the house?'

'It needs to be done. I've got to get back to New York; I've got commitments to meet.'

'Of course.'

There was silence for a moment, as if neither of them knew what to say next. It was Annie who broke it.

'So what are you doing here?'

'I had a chapter meeting in town and while I'm here I thought I'd call in and see if I can arrange a second viewing at The Priory. On my own this time, to fix my ideas of what we could do with it, take some photos. You know how easy it is to forget details.'

'Good idea,' Annie nodded. 'Well, I'll be seeing you. There's so much to sort out at home; I've got to make a start somewhere.'

She was halfway to the door when he said, 'Annie, would you like to come along? You're a photographer, I could use you.'

'Don't you want to know my rates first?' she quipped.

'Oh,' his face fell.

'Don't be silly.' She grinned. 'Yes, I'll come along. I'll take some photos for you. It'll be nice to feel useful again.'

'Shall I ring you later then?' he perked up again. 'I'll make arrangements to pick you up tomorrow.'

'That'll be fine.'

She wondered as she drove home why she'd been so ready to agree to the idea, why The Priory should have such a hold over her after everything that had happened there. Surely it couldn't have anything to do with Tim Raven-wood? The very thought of it made her smile. Don't be ridiculous — he was a vicar!

5

The following afternoon the vicar picked her up in his old Renault. She noticed the books scattered over the back seat — songbooks, a book of prayers, a tattered bible. In the footwell there were a stack of CDs, most of secular bands which surprised Annie.

'You know we could have walked,' she suggested. 'It's a nice day and The Priory isn't too far.'

'Force of habit I'm afraid. I'm usually so busy I don't have the luxury of walking. I could do with more exercise,' he patted his stomach which to Annie didn't appear in the slightest bit flabby. 'So, once your house is on the market you'll be leaving I guess?'

'It could take months to sell and I can't hang around that long,' she agreed. 'My mother's old friend, Val Linton, has agreed to keep an eye on things for me.'

'You haven't considered staying?'

'No.' Not once had it crossed her mind.

'I don't suppose Chattelcombe can compare to Manhattan.' He grinned. 'And you enjoy your work.'

'Love it.' She stroked the camera in her lap. 'What about you?'

'Yep.' He nodded.

'I've never known a vicar before.' Annie watched the hawthorn hedges speed past as they hit the country lanes leading out of the village. 'You don't just work on Sundays then?'

'I wish!' He laughed.

He told her about some of the things that made up his usual working week — administration, visits, services, funerals, preparation, meetings, interviews for weddings and baptisms, counselling — the list seemed to go on and on.

'Not forgetting,' he said as the open gates of The Priory appeared ahead, 'purchasing country mansions.'

Annie couldn't help but tense as the car growled up the drive. If Tim sensed it he didn't comment. The estate agent was waiting for them on the steps to the main entrance.

'Just take your time,' he said as Tim shook his hand. 'I'll wait out here.'

As they disappeared inside he pulled out a packet of cigarettes and lit up.

The hall was silent and cavernous now there were only two of them. Once again Annie's gaze was drawn to the stairs yet the memory didn't have the same effect this time — that image of Edward was replaced with the Edward she'd dined with the other night: the older, corporeal Edward Nunce, the Edward of the now, not of the past.

'Alright?'

Tim's enquiry jolted her out of her reverie.

'Fine.' She smiled. 'Where do you want to start?' She pulled the camera out of its casing.

Annie followed Tim from room to room, clicking away with her camera. As he enthused about what could be done with the house it began to take on a different ambience.

'The dining room is the biggest. I think we might turn that into a chapel. How many en-suite bedrooms do you think we could have?'

As she saw the house through his eyes she began to see its potential, not its past.

'Ah Annie.' He sighed. 'My vision is not just to get in well-heeled Christians who want a week of spiritual refreshment. I want to reach out to people with real problems, people from all walks of life, people we can help.'

'I think the house would appreciate that,' she said.

He shot her a pleased look.

'All we need to do now is clinch it,' he said.

'That's going to take a miracle,' Annie muttered.

'They do happen you know.'

She'd never seen any evidence of it.

'Are you done with the photographs?' she asked.

'I think we've got enough.'

She excused herself and went back out into the sunshine. The estate agent was now on his mobile phone, pushing around gravel with the toe of his shoe as he jabbered away into the handset.

Annie turned in the opposite direction, walking along the front of the house towards the ruins.

Hollyhocks, lupins and poppies nodded under the windows, fighting for space among the mass of tangled weeds. The grass was beginning to grow wild on the other side of the path where the Old Priory's south wall stood. The sun shone directly onto the old, honeyed stone.

Something moved and Annie stood still. She drew in a gasp as she saw a shadow flit across a gap exactly where she'd seen it before — and this time she saw a flash of a blue dress and dark hair. There was no mistaking it.

She turned around and hurried back to the house. Tim was coming down the steps. His smile of satisfaction turned to concern when he saw her.

'Are you alright? You look as if you've seen a ghost.'

'Perhaps I have,' Annie put a hand to her chest then shook her head as Tim came near. 'No, don't worry. It's a trick of the light, you know what old ruins are like.'

He wasn't so easily appeased.

'Is there something you need to say?' He looked at her shrewdly. 'Something from the past you need to resolve?'

'No, it's nothing.' She examined her camera. Why hadn't she thought of taking a photo?

★   ★   ★

As her laptop didn't have the facility to print, and her mother certainly didn't possess a computer, Annie agreed to go back to the vicarage to download the photos onto Tim's computer. Tim made coffee then invited her into his study. She looked around as he sat at a desk covered in papers. There were shelves of books and photographs of family and

90

friends, of places he'd been (she recognised Machu Pichu), smiley faces of South American children, an ordination photograph with what she assumed were his proud parents at his side. In one corner stood a guitar, a bulky photocopier occupied another. On one wall hung a poster of a very Jewish-looking, muscular Jesus. A wooden cross stood on the window-sill.

Annie didn't know what to feel in a room whose ethos was entirely different to what she was used to. On one level she felt uncomfortable, yet on another she recognised it from her childhood. It was something she'd left behind. When? After Charlotte's accident? She felt she didn't deserve to be in church surrounded by good people. Definitely after Edward's betrayal; the death of expectation and faith.

The fact that Tim possessed both expectation and faith in bucketloads made her feel good, she realised. If someone like him could give his whole life to it perhaps there was some substance to it after all.

'Right, I'm connected now,' he said, shaking her out of her thoughts. 'Here we go.'

She perched on the arm of the old armchair at the side of his desk and sipped on her coffee as he downloaded the photos she'd shot.

'I'll print them later,' he said as he sat back in his chair when they'd finished. 'I might design a pamphlet for the committee and the diocese. Thanks Annie. A good afternoon's work.'

'Yeah,' she agreed. 'Thanks for asking me to come.'

Their eyes locked for a moment. She looked away.

'You've got a lot of photos,' she said quickly. 'Who's this?'

She pointed to a photograph showing a young woman standing behind him, one arm draped about his neck, the two of them carefree and laughing.

'That's Clare,' he said. 'She and I were an item for a while.'

'What happened?'

'She got cancer and died.'

'Oh, I'm sorry.'

'It was six years ago.'

'What did that do to your faith?' Annie couldn't resist asking him the intrusive question.

'You know, she had the most tremendous faith,' he smiled reflectively. 'She was ready to go at the end and she knew where she was going. It was a horrendous time but it was also wonderful. I don't know if you can understand that?'

Annie wasn't sure she could.

'She was one of the people who influenced me to go into the ministry.'

'Has there been anyone else since?'

'Not really.'

'A lot to live up to.' Annie placed her empty mug on the desk.

'Maybe.'

'I had dinner with Edward the other night,' she said suddenly.

'Oh,' Tim looked surprised.

'For old times' sake. I don't think he realises how much he hurt me. He started talking about missed opportunities, opportunities coming around again. I don't know,' she shrugged. 'You can't go back, can you?'

'I certainly haven't found a way to do it,' he smiled, hands clasped across his abdomen.

'I think I'd better go,' Annie uncurled herself from the arm of the chair — her legs were stiff. 'You must have lots of work to be getting on with, and I've got a house to get ready for sale. Thanks for the coffee.'

'Thanks for the photos.'

★   ★   ★

The house felt unwelcoming when she returned, as if it knew she was about to divest it of all that made it a home. But it hadn't been her home for so long. There were very few of her personal effects there — her mother had long ago cleared out her bedroom. She thought of Tim's study with all his personal things. Then she thought of her apartment in New York.

She looked at her watch — Jessica would be at work now. She rang her cellphone and was pleased to hear her friend's American drawl on the other end of the line.

'Hi Annie. What's up?'

She told her about the funeral, about the house, about The Priory and seeing Edward again, and about Tim and his plans for a retreat centre.

'Cute vicar, eh?' Jessica teased.

'I didn't say he was cute.'

'I could hear it in your voice.'

'Well don't get any ideas. I'll be heading home soon. There are a few things I need to get sorted out first.'

'Okay Annie. Well, don't take too long. I miss you. The apartment's too quiet without you!'

Annie felt much better after talking to Jessica. She had another life somewhere else and would soon be able to leave

behind all the complications of Chattelcombe.

★ ★ ★

She slept fitfully that night, her dreams
inhabited by visions of Charlotte in her
blue dress. Charlotte crying, Charlotte
insisting, 'I'm going to tell Daddy!'
Charlotte losing her footing and falling.
And finally — and most vividly
— Charlotte whimpering, calling for
her father who never came.

Annie woke in a cold sweat. She felt
her heart would break. Where was the
professor? Why hadn't he come? And,
crazily, why did that weigh so heavily on
her? What was this sudden feeling of
responsibility? There was nothing she
could have done about it.

As she lay there in the dark, she
played over the events of that fateful
day again, remembered Mrs Nunce
asking, 'What happened Edward? Tell
me what happened?'

'Charlie slipped and fell,' Edward

answered calmly.

'And what were you doing? Were you teasing her, Edward? Were you playing properly?'

'Yes, we were playing a proper game. She slipped on the step and fell. Ask Annie.'

Mrs Nunce's fearful eyes had been turned on her. 'Yes, Mrs Nunce, Charlotte slipped and fell,' Annie had confirmed. Part of her had wanted to say that they had been running away from her, that Edward had pushed her, but that would have got him into trouble, would have got her into trouble too; but she was more concerned for Edward.

The next day Edward had sat her down in their den in the rhododendron bushes near the estate wall. 'You're my best friend Annie. You're my secret keeper. You must never say what happened. It was Charlie's fault anyway.'

'How could it have been Charlotte's fault, Edward?' she'd protested loudly, looking right at him.

'Make a promise now, Annie. Make a promise to be my secret keeper forever. It'll be you and me forever.' She liked the sound of that so she made the promise.

Of course, once Charlotte regained consciousness the truth came out and Annie felt guilty for ever backing Edward. Then the professor had taken her aside and said gravely, 'Annie, we don't want you to speak of this. It was an accident, we're agreed.' And she was happy to acquiesce. She understood that the family had a reputation to preserve, but it had cost them — particularly Charlotte.

Annie brushed a tear away, amazed that something that happened so long ago still had a powerful effect. Maybe it was the shock of discovering that Charlotte had recently died. Was Charlotte still at The Priory? An unresting soul? Was that her ghost Annie had seen, even though she didn't believe in ghosts?

Edward had spoken of opportunities

the other night. Perhaps he was right. Perhaps this was an opportunity to be reconciled to the past. Even the vicar had picked up on it when he asked if there was something from the past that needed to be resolved.

That question suddenly felt sharply pertinent as she went downstairs to make a cup of tea. Not just about Charlotte. There were things she needed to resolve about her past here too, about her mother. Something wasn't quite right and she didn't know what.

* * *

Someone from the estate agency called the following day to take some photographs and make a valuation on the property.

'I have every confidence this will sell quickly,' he said.

'Even with the work that needs to be done?' Annie sounded dubious.

'Chattelcombe is a desirable location.

Provided you don't want top dollar, it won't be a sitter.'

No, Annie didn't want the best price; she wanted to be rid of it.

★   ★   ★

On Sunday morning Annie went to church. She sat at the back until Teresa saw her and invited her to join her family nearer the front. Annie couldn't refuse.

Tim spotted her straightaway and favoured her with a wink and a smile. It was the first church service she'd been to in years — apart from her mother's funeral — and different to what she'd experienced with Father Jacobs. It was light-hearted with hymns that swung and the children were invited to make their contribution. The sermon wasn't boring either. Annie began to feel a little less of an outsider. She thought Tim looked rather handsome in his long white robes and colourful stole.

Coffee was served after the service in the hall next door.

'Tim showed us the photos you took the other day,' Teresa said.

'You didn't mind me going with him, did you?'

'Why should I mind?'

'I'm not a member of the church. I'm not really involved in the project. It's just that we bumped into each other in the estate agents and he invited me. I had a skill he could use.'

'I think you're more involved than you imagine, Annie.' Teresa smiled at her knowingly.

Annie looked across the hall to where Tim was meeting and greeting with a cup of coffee in his hand. He seemed totally at home as he laughed with a small group of people. For a brief moment she felt a searing pain. 'Where do I belong?' she thought before allowing herself to be drawn back into the conversation around her.

Eventually Tim worked his way around to her.

'I'm glad you came,' he smiled. 'What did you think?'

'It's certainly different to how I remember church,' Annie replied.

'Good.'

'Terrible sermon though,' she quipped.

'I'll do much better if you come again next week,' he chuckled, getting her humour.

'I'll think about it.'

'By the way, the churchwardens and I will be meeting with the diocesan architect this week to draw up preliminary plans for The Priory,' he informed her. 'Once we've got drawings we can put them on display with your photos and hopefully generate some extra funds. Have you heard anything further from Edward Nunce? I don't think he's put in an offer yet.'

'No, not a word,' Annie confessed.

She felt confused by Edward's lack of communication after he'd appeared to be so keen to see her again. Then again, she shouldn't have been surprised; Edward always did his own thing. She wasn't even sure she wanted him to get in touch again. The past was best left alone.

'Are you free Tuesday evening?' Teresa interjected, drawing Annie's thoughts away from Edward.

She was free every night.

'Good. You and Tim can come around for a meal again.'

Tim shrugged and grinned at her. Obviously he was used to being steamrollered by Teresa.

'I think he likes you,' Teresa whispered after he'd moved away.

'No,' Annie protested. But as she considered the possibility it wasn't an unwelcome thought.

★ ★ ★

Annie had just got back from Sunday lunch with Val Linton when the phone rang. Her heart skipped a beat when she realised it was Edward.

'Hi Annie. Sorry I haven't been in touch. I had to come back to London, business to see to.'

'I wasn't waiting for your call,' she lied.

'You're telling me you've got a life, I know.'

She pulled a face because he couldn't see it.

'I'm coming down to Chattelcombe this week. My surveyor's coming with me to look over The Priory before I make an offer on it. Can we meet up?'

'I'm actually seeing someone on Tuesday evening.' Annie felt the need to inform him.

'A date?'

'Tim Ravenwood, the vicar.'

A pause on the other end of the line.

'Well Annie, you certainly are full of surprises,' he said eventually. 'I wouldn't have matched you up with a vicar.'

It wasn't a date of course; she wasn't 'seeing' Tim. She was using it as a barricade against Edward because she realised she was vulnerable to his charms, because she didn't want him to think she was still in love with him.

'I'll make a note in my diary,' he continued. ' 'Tuesday evening is out. Date with the vicar.' '

Annie felt a flash of anger at the amusement in his voice.

'I'm thinking Wednesday morning,' he said. 'Why don't we meet at The Priory? Let's get back on common ground, the place where we were closest. Stu and I will be there at ten. I'll let him get on with the business and we can reminisce, connect again perhaps.'

He knew how to get her. To be there again with Edward, to revisit old, shared places — the pull was irresistible, even though she knew it probably wasn't the wisest thing to do. What had she said to Tim the other day, 'Can we ever go back to the past?' Despite all that, she found herself agreeing.

'I'll meet you there,' she said.

'I'll look forward to it.'

He certainly sounded genuine. Maybe he was, Annie reflected as she wandered into the sitting room and began sorting through the piles of old magazines and books. Maybe he really did regret the past, maybe he was alone, maybe they were meant to be together. She shook her head to clear it; it was all too confusing.

6

Annie felt confused. Edward had kissed her, had implied he wanted to be with her. Isn't that what she'd always wanted? Except she wasn't that 19-year-old student anymore and too much had happened down the years since then. She hardly knew him. What had happened after his divorce? Surely he hadn't lived like a hermit all those years? For all she knew he could have a wife or a steady girlfriend back in London and this was just a tantalising fling for him.

Worst of all had been the look on Tim's face. He'd been on the way to share the outcome of the meeting with the architect with her and that kiss from Edward had stopped him in his tracks and turned him around. She felt she'd let him down and couldn't believe how much it mattered to her.

Why did Tim have to appear at that precise moment? Why couldn't it have been ten minutes later when Edward was gone and she would have been home alone?

Annie barely slept again that night, wondering what Edward was going to do next. Would he call? Where would it lead if he did? And the next morning, because Tim was still on her mind and she felt she couldn't call on him, she went into the village and sought out Teresa in the flower shop.

'Well, hello!' her friend greeted her from behind tall green vases of sunflowers and sweet williams on the counter. 'This is a nice surprise.'

'What would you recommend?' Annie looked around at the buckets of flowers and foliage on the tiled floor. 'Something to cheer up the house. Now it's on the market I'd better do something about its ambience.'

'Fresh coffee and bake your own bread,' Teresa put down her scissors and came out from behind the counter.

'Failing that, I always find ranunculus cheerful,' she indicated the rounded pink, yellow, orange and cream blooms near the door. 'And sunflowers will cheer anyone up. How much do you want to spend? A vase of gladioli in the hallway will make a bold statement.'

'Yeah, go on, all of them.' Annie sighed and sat on the stool in front of the counter.

'Oh, oh, that sigh sounds ominous,' Teresa brought the selected flowers to the counter and laid them out on top of thick paper.

'Something happened yesterday,' Annie confessed and proceeded to tell her friend about her meeting at The Priory with Edward, watching as Teresa efficiently snipped off the end of the stems and tied the bunches of flowers together.

'What does he want?' she asked shrewdly when her friend paused to draw breath.

'I'm not sure really. He talks about going back to the past, of missed opportunities.'

Teresa screwed up her mouth. 'Yeah, I bet he does.'

'What's that supposed to mean?' Annie shot her a sharp look.

'It's just, I never really liked him in school. I know you were all over him — the two of you had something going on,' she began to wrap the flowers, cutting tape off the dispenser with a practised swish and tear, 'but he could be quite nasty sometimes. And a bit of a snob because he lived at the big house and was so good looking.'

'Oh, I wasn't aware of it.'

'He used to enjoy pulling my hair.' Teresa shrugged. 'And he wasn't very nice to his sister, he always seemed to be teasing her.'

Annie concentrated on watching her friend fix the paper wrapping with a final flourish of tape.

'And now he's back, Mr Arrogant Big Shot, thinking he can get The Priory. And he probably can — we're minnows compared to him.'

'I didn't know you disliked him so

much.' Annie looked up.

'How I feel isn't important,' Teresa said. 'Nor is it important what Edward Nunce wants. The important thing Annie is — what do you want?'

Annie bit her lip.

Teresa leaned on her hands on the counter.

'I thought you and Tim got on really well the other night,' she said. 'You seemed relaxed, you seemed to enjoy his company. Picking up on the vibes — and he hasn't said anything to me, mind — I think he likes you.'

'Oh Teresa.' Annie sighed. 'I really don't want to lose his friendship but I'm afraid I might.' Annie sighed again, a deep, heavy sigh this time and told her friend about how Tim had caught Edward kissing her the previous day. 'Now he must think I'm consorting with the enemy. One day I'm with him at The Priory, taking photos and enthusing over his plans, and a few days later I'm there with Edward, his arch-rival.'

'Do you want Edward to get The Priory?'

'No,' Annie said. 'Not after what happened; he doesn't deserve it.'

'What happened?' Teresa said quickly and Annie realised that she'd said too much.

'I mean the family history,' Annie tried her best to smooth over the slip. 'Charlotte's accident, the way the family fell apart afterwards. It became a really sad place. I think a retreat centre, a place to help people, would be better for it.'

'What if Edward wants the two of you to be together and to live there?'

'I don't . . . I couldn't . . . ' Annie trailed off, unable to contemplate making it her home.

'Oh Annie, you've got more than you bargained for coming home,' Teresa lay a sympathetic hand on her arm.

'How much for the flowers?' Annie slid off the stool and reached into her bag for her purse.

'For you . . . '

'No.' She raised a hand. 'Full price. It's your business.'

'Fifteen pounds.'

Annie handed over the money and scooped the flowers into her arms.

'Can you let Tim know I'm still in the project?' she said as she was about to leave. 'I don't know what's happening with Edward, but I don't want to lose Tim's friendship and respect — it's meant so much to me since my mother's death.'

'You should tell him yourself.'

'No.' Annie shook her head. 'It's too presumptuous.'

★ ★ ★

Annie was busy arranging the flowers when the door knocker sounded. She deposited a vase of gladioli on the hall table on the way to answer it, a feeling of relief and pleasure sweeping over her, certain it would be Tim. But she opened the door to Edward.

'Oh!' she said, thrown by his presence.

'Not expecting it to be me, obviously,' he remarked drolly. 'Did you think it was your vicar friend?'

'What are you doing here?'

'We have things to talk about. Can I come in?'

Without waiting for an answer he walked through into the sitting room.

'It's in a mess,' she apologised. 'I'm getting it ready for sale.'

'I remember your mother, Annie.' He picked up a fussy, crocheted cushion and inspected it. 'She always wanted to be someone. She was glad you got friendly with us, it gave her access to that world.'

'I'd rather you weren't so deprecatory about her; she's only just died.'

'I'm sorry.' He tossed the cushion down again, came towards her and, taking her hands in his said, 'You're getting rid of your past. Let's forget mine. Let's make something new together.'

The smell of him was enticing and just as she was about to fall into him the phone rang.

'I'd better get it,' she said.

It was Paul, her estate agent.

'I've got a couple of viewings tomorrow,' she told Edward when she came back to the sitting room.

'And I wanted to take you out for the day.' Edward was used to getting what he wanted.

'It'll have to be another time,' she said. 'I have to get rid of the house, I have to get back to New York.'

'You don't have to do anything Annie.'

'I can ask Paul to show them around I suppose,' she ruminated.

'Good girl,' he clasped her by the back of the head drawing her close and kissed her forehead. 'I'll pick you up at eleven.'

'You're not staying? I thought you said we had to talk.'

'We'll do it tomorrow. I've got business to take care of. See you then.'

And then he was gone, like a whirlwind, changing her plans and planting expectations again.

The following day they drove to a seafood restaurant a little way down the coast and ordered lunch. Edward told her about his business interests, she spoke of her photographic career.

'Is your mother still alive?' Annie asked.

'Yes, she lives just outside Sydney.' Edward twirled his fork. 'I went back for Charlie's funeral but apart from that I never see her. She's settled with a new partner.'

'And what about you?'

'I told you, Natasha and I split up after a year. No children.'

'There must have been someone in the years since then.'

'Girlfriends have come and gone. Perhaps nobody measured up to you.'

'If that had been true you wouldn't have married Natasha,' Annie remarked tartly.

After lunch was over he drove her back to the outskirts of the village and, leaving the car at the top of the cliff, they negotiated the steep, gorse-lined path down to the small cove where they'd often played as children.

The light glistening off the sea and the somnolent shushing of the waves made Annie feel as if she was in a magic land, a place where time stood still.

They walked side by side across the width of the bay, dodging the incoming tide.

'We used to do this when we were kids,' he laughed.

'We used to hide from Charlotte,' Annie remembered, 'in that cave over there,' she pointed to the far side of the cove. 'Do you remember?'

'Why do you always have to bring Charlie into it?' His tone slid from happy reminiscing into irritation.

Annie stopped walking.

'Because she was part of it all,' she looked into Edward's brooding eyes. 'You can't get away from that.'

'There was a time after Charlie's accident, you know. We had years after

Charlie,' he said defensively.

'But she sort of defined our relationship, didn't she? I became your secret keeper; there was more at stake afterwards. From that time on I felt bound to you.' *Until you broke those bonds in Cambridge* she thought.

'Don't you ever think about it Edward? Surely you can't have dealt with it, just like that? We were children. An incident like that stays in the psyche for a long time.'

'In yours perhaps,' he continued walking and she hurried to catch up with him.

'I haven't felt right since I've been back,' Annie confessed. 'I never had a chance to put things right with her. I let her down. Her dreams were destroyed, and no-one was totally honest about what happened that day. Sometimes I feel I want to tell someone.'

'Annie,' he stopped, cupped her face in his hands and gazed intently into her eyes. 'It's in the past. Let it go.'

Then, in an attempt to erase any

unpleasant memories, he kissed her, a long, powerful, demanding kiss. Only when they both felt the sea around their ankles did they spring apart.

'Come on!' He laughed. He kicked off his shoes and socks, rolled up his trousers, and splashed into the sea.

Annie kicked off her sandals and followed.

Yes, she thought. *I remember doing this*.

But afterwards, when they'd returned to the car and were on their way home, she reflected on how the afternoon had been about the past, of how Edward had chosen what they were going to do and she had followed once again, of how he'd headed off any discussion about Charlotte and what had happened all those years ago. Maybe he had dealt with it, but Annie was discovering that she hadn't.

'I've got to go back to London tomorrow,' he said when they drew up outside the house. He leaned close, ran a finger over her cheek. 'I could stay here for the night, or you could come back to The George,' he whispered in her ear.

'I don't think so,' Annie moved away. 'I'm not that easy.'

Edward chuckled.

'That's the girl I remember.' He placed his hands back on the steering wheel and stared ahead through the windscreen. 'Well Annie, am I coming back again?'

'That's up to you.'

His lip curled in a smile.

'I think I might.'

She opened the car door.

'Remember,' he said, 'you're my secret keeper.'

She waved and watched him as he drove away. That night her dreams were dark and lurid again.

★　★　★

Annie felt it would be hypocritical to go to church on Sunday morning so she stayed away. She was surprised, therefore, to get a phone call from Tim later that afternoon.

'We missed you this morning,' he said. He sounded perfectly normal — chatty and friendly with no edge to his voice.

'I slept late.' She hated lying.

'Well, I thought you might like to know that there's a meeting in the hall about The Priory on Tuesday at seven,' he informed her. 'I hope you'll be able to come.'

'I'm on your side, you know,' she felt compelled to tell him.

'So I'll expect you there then?'

After that Annie had no alternative but to go. The hall was packed with eager parishioners, curious to learn of the latest developments. At the front of the room stood a display of preliminary drawings, costings and the photographs she'd taken the other day. Tim sat behind a table along with the steering committee.

Seeing Teresa halfway down, Annie went to join her.

'I was wondering whether you'd turn

up,' her friend moved her bag from the chair next to her. 'I saved one just in case.'

'Tim rang and asked me to come,' Annie said as she sat down. She regarded Teresa through suspicious eyes. 'You didn't have anything to do with that, did you?'

Teresa didn't have time to answer as Tim stood up and brought the meeting to order.

There followed a lively discussion about the possible ways of using the house including some interesting ideas on how the ruins might be utilised too. Only when Tim updated them on how far short of the asking price they still were did the mood in the room deflate.

'What can we do?' someone asked.

'The parish is having a gift day this coming Sunday,' Tim said. 'But whatever happens we're going to put in an offer — any offer is better than no offer at all.'

'What about Edward Nunce?' somebody else piped up.

'As far as I understand it, he hasn't put an offer in yet.'

Annie felt herself flush as Tim said it, hoping he wouldn't look at her.

'Perhaps he'll change his mind,' came a voice from the back of the hall.

'We can certainly pray about it.' Tim grinned.

Refreshments were served after the meeting closed. Annie sauntered across to the display boards while Teresa busied herself with serving coffee and biscuits.

'They came out well.'

She turned to see Tim at her side. He nodded at the photographs.

'I'm glad you could use them,' she took a quick sip of her coffee; it was hot and burnt her tongue. At her side Tim exhaled a contemplative sigh. 'I'm sorry about the other day,' she blurted out.

'No worries,' he smiled, crinkling the edges of his kind eyes.

'It was rather sudden,' she explained.

'Are you two a couple now?'

'I . . . I don't know.'

'The reason why I ask is because I don't want you to compromise yourself Annie.'

'What do you mean?'

'If you and Edward Nunce are together, and it's his intention to buy Chattelcombe Priory, then you'll have to support him.'

Annie didn't know what she wanted she realised as she looked at Tim, so calm and dependable at her side. He was dressed in jeans and a short-sleeved blue clerical shirt that mirrored the colour of his eyes. His black hair looked unkempt and a little on the long side and, by this time of the day, there was a dark shadow along his jawline.

There was no side to Tim — she could feel the integrity at the core of him and in that moment she longed to be able to tell him everything that had happened; she had the feeling he wouldn't be shocked nor judgemental; she sensed he would be a rock.

'Vicar, Kim Dalton's got a brilliant fundraising idea,' a plump, middle-aged woman tapped him on the arm.

'Great, all ideas welcome!' Tim said and excused himself from Annie with a wink.

She watched him disappear into the huddle of ladies. Then she finished her coffee, looked at the board one more time and announced to Teresa that she was going home.

* * *

Nothing had come of the viewings from the previous week. She spoke to Paul who said, 'They both quite liked the house, but not enough to make an offer. I think you'll get more of a positive response once it's been emptied.'

It was just the jolt Annie needed. She rang Val Linton and asked her if she could spare some time to help her finish the job of sorting through her mother's things.

'Take whatever you want from the house Val,' Annie said as she started sifting through the colourful china in the tall display cabinet. 'My mother was such a hoarder. I think I'll be here until this time next year trying to sort everything out.'

'It's a pity you're selling up, losing ties with Chattelcombe. Won't you ever come back?' The older woman examined a pile of magazines that Annie had merely shifted from one corner of the living room to another.

'Never say never,' Annie said, turning her attention to the shelves in the alcove next to the fireplace. 'Do you know anyone who wants books?'

'The charity shop?' Val offered.

They weren't Annie's sort of books — mostly sagas and romances. There were some travelogues dotted amongst them and they might have been interesting except they served to remind Annie that her mother had never really travelled — only once had she been to visit Annie in New York and had declared that she didn't like the food and missed her bed.

She pulled them out one by one, depositing them in a box. As the shelves emptied it revealed a book flush with the wall, with a red cover and a ribboned marker. There was no inscription on the front.

Intrigued, Annie picked it up and opened it to discover pages in her mother's handwriting. It was a diary. Some of the ink had bled into the lines but not so that it was indecipherable. She glanced at the date scrawled across the top of a page and recognised it as a time just after she'd met Edward and Charlotte. Curious to know what her mother had thought of it, she began to read.

William called. I'd sent Annie to the shop. We didn't have long, but what a thrill, knowing she could come back and catch us at any moment.

William. She grimaced at the deceit. She'd had no idea her mother had been seeing someone. But then she supposed she must have had some boyfriends over the years, having been widowed at a young age. Annie turned to another page.

I love the fact that he's so studious. It's like he's studying me. And who would have believed a man so precise and so meticulous could show so much passion!

Annie pulled a face. It was difficult to think of her mother showing sexual passion. Was she in love? Why had her mother never introduced this man?

On to another page where she found the answer to her questions.

We had a row. I hate it when he has to go home! Why can't he leave his family for me? Doesn't he love me? Don't I deserve more? Oh William, I want so much more!

Annie sat down on the arm of the comfortable chair by the fireplace, running a finger across her bottom lip as she continued to read, part of her wanting to stop, the stronger part morbidly fascinated by the knowledge that her mother had been a mistress and wanting to know more.

She came across some purple prose on a particularly torrid afternoon, quickly skipping over it to follow the entry on the adjacent page.

God in heaven! All hell has broken loose. Charlotte has had an accident. They couldn't find William. He wasn't at the college because he was here with me, and now Iris knows something is up.

Annie gasped.

'What's the matter?' Val looked up.

Annie turned the page. She knew what she would find there.

My poor William. Charlotte is in a bad way and he is heartbroken. I want to comfort him but I can't see him. He won't come to me. What am I to do? My life is over if I can't see him anymore!

Annie couldn't read any further. She snapped the diary shut. Everything was swimming around in her head.

7

Annie continued to stare at the diary in her lap. Her mother and William Nunce! Now she understood why the professor was nowhere to be found when Charlotte was calling for him. Those cries still haunted Annie. And she'd never been able to understand why, after Charlotte's accident, her mother had been even more hateful towards her, Annie had thought that perhaps her's and Edward's secret was out and her mother was punishing her for it. Finally it all made sense; William Nunce had been so guilt-ridden and broken-hearted he'd given her up. Resenting Annie's continuing relationship with Edward had driven her mother to outright hostility at times.

Annie recalled how one day her mother had approached the professor in the village, trying to offer comfort, but

William Nunce had shaken her hand off his arm with a degree of vehemence that had caused people walking by to draw back in shock.

'Oh God,' Annie breathed out as she remembered the occasions her mother had furtively slipped her a note when she'd been about to go up to The Priory.

'Annie,' she'd smiled and spoken lovingly at those times. 'Pass this letter on to the professor for me. It's something he's asked me to do. Don't tell anyone, though, he wants it to be a secret so try and do it when nobody's looking.'

The professor had frowned at her as she'd pushed the paper into his hand. Once he'd shouted at her and she'd been scared, so fearsome did he look in his grief.

'I don't want any more notes! Tell your mother to just leave me alone!'

And then Annie'd had to suffer a tongue-lashing from her mother as she'd delivered the message, puzzled as to why simply obeying instructions could possibly provoke such rage in two people.

Val looked at her as she sighed.

'Did you know about this?' Annie held up the book. 'My mother kept a diary; she wrote about her affair with Professor Nunce.'

Val's cheeks coloured.

'You did? Why didn't you tell me?'

Val straightened up from her crouching position on the floor. 'You were a child,' she said, 'You wouldn't have understood these things. Anyway, it brought nothing but unhappiness to the both of them. William Nunce went into a decline after his daughter's accident, his marriage broke up, and I'm afraid your mother became even more bitter. I can't say she enjoyed life.'

'No, and she took it out on me. Didn't you ever try to dissuade her?'

'You know your mother,' Val smiled wryly. 'Once her mind was set on something it was impossible to talk her out of it.' Val placed a sympathetic hand on Annie's shoulder. 'I'm sorry. This must all be very difficult for you.'

Annie sighed and gazed at the book in her lap. Things were suddenly falling into place; she knew why she thought she'd been seeing Charlotte up at the ruins lately, why she'd been feeling culpable. She hadn't been honest. She'd kept quiet all these years.

More than that, Annie had been ignorant of how her own family had been deeply caught up in the tragedy, bound to the Nunces.

Suddenly she knew what she had to do.

'I have to speak to Tim,' she said as she slid off the chair and put the diary in her bag.

'Is it wise to dredge up the past?' Val looked concerned.

'In this case, yes,' Annie answered firmly as she walked towards the living room door. 'There's something I need to do.'

★ ★ ★

Tim picked up the agitation in her voice when she rang and told her to come over to the vicarage right away.

'Do you want me to carry on while you're gone?' Val offered.

'No,' Annie said. She didn't know what state she'd be in when she came home, whether she'd want to face her mother's friend.

Val nodded, understanding.

'Give me a ring when you need me again,' she said. 'Any time you want to talk, I'm here for you.'

Annie swung her bag onto her shoulder and started out for the vicarage. As she walked she thought about Edward. She'd never breathed a word about what had happened. Now she was about to break that promise.

'What's happened?' Tim asked as he opened the door, a look of concern on his face. 'You sounded strange on the phone.'

'I've just discovered something about my past, something that changes everything. You're the only one I could think of to talk to. Have you got time to listen?'

'All the time you need Annie,' his words were like balm and Annie had to blink away the tears that sprung to her eyes.

He made coffee then Annie followed him into the study. She sat down in the battered armchair, cradling the coffee mug in her hands as she looked around at his happy photographs, at the cross on the window and the picture of the very human Christ. Was she guilty? She wondered. Could she be forgiven?

'Now, what is it?'

She turned her attention back to him. His blue eyes were serious yet full of kindness.

'What you said at The Priory the other day, about things needing to be resolved,' she began, feeling her way carefully. 'You were right.'

He nodded encouragement.

'Certain things happened in the past that I've told no-one about. I promised Edward and the Nunce family I wouldn't; we made a pact. And then this afternoon, when clearing out the house, I found this.' Annie put her coffee aside and drew the diary out of her bag but didn't offer it to him. 'It's a diary, kept by my mother.' She ran her fingers over the cover. 'What I've found written in here changes everything. It explains the way I've been feeling.' She looked at Tim hopefully. 'Priests aren't supposed to share things told in confidence are they?'

'The confessional is sacrosanct,' he confirmed.

Annie suddenly realised that she dreaded his judgement, that this could change his opinion of her, but she'd come too far to back out now. She felt she owed it to Charlotte. So it all came spilling out: her history with Edward, her mother's affair with the professor, and then — finally — that fateful day when Edward had pushed his sister and the secret pact she'd made with him afterwards.

'We've always said it was an accident,' she finished. 'I colluded with him. He called me his secret keeper. I loved him even then. He always had the power to make me follow him.'

'Did he intend to cause his sister harm?' Tim asked carefully.

'No, I don't think he did. He was mean to her sometimes — I think he resented that I was her friend too; he wanted to take me away from her. But we were playing a game that day and he just pushed her out of the way. He would never have deliberately harmed her.'

'Then it was an accident,' Tim said. 'But his fear made him cover the whole thing up. Don't forget Annie, you were both children at the time.'

Annie nodded. 'I think his greatest fear was that, if his parents found out, he wouldn't be loved anymore. His father was always cold towards him — it was Charlotte who was the apple of the professor's eye.' Annie laced her fingers together and studied them.

'Of course, when Charlotte regained consciousness it all came tumbling out. It was her word against his and she won because it was the truth. Edward was punished — I don't know how but he was subdued for a long time. And then the professor took me aside and made me swear not to tell anyone — they didn't want the stigma. Well, I'd already sworn to Edward.

'And now today I discovered this link between my mother and the family. I can't seem to get away from it. I haven't been sleeping well since I've been home — partly because of my mother's death, I know, but also because Charlotte's been on my mind. Now I know why. When I think of her calling for her father when she needed him most and him not being there because he was with my mother . . . Ugh! It disgusts me!'

She looked at Tim, dreading seeing that feeling of disgust reflected in his eyes, but they revealed only understanding and compassion. She wondered in that moment how she could have over-looked him for Edward.

'You'll probably think I'm mad,' she continued tentatively. 'But I think I've seen Charlotte at The Priory — her ghost, her spirit, call it what you will. I found out from Edward she died recently in a car accident. I think she's been trying to speak to me. Am I mad?'

'Sometimes these things happen for a reason,' Tim said calmly. 'You've come back to Chattelcombe, so has Edward Nunce. It's not so much about Charlotte as about the two of you. There are things from the past which need to be laid to rest in order for you to move on.'

It made sense. Had she ever been able to get away from Edward and her past? She thought of Benton and the others before him, how in every relationship she'd ever had she knew she'd been partly absent.

'It's just such a relief to be able to tell someone after all of these years,' Annie confessed.

'But this isn't the end of it.'

For a moment Annie thought he was going to betray her, break the confessional after all.

'You now have to talk to Edward about all of this,' Tim advised. 'And then I think we need to go back to The Priory and bring things to a close once and for all.'

★ ★ ★

The only problem was, Annie had no way of getting in touch with Edward. He hadn't left her a phone number and when she contacted the estate agent they refused to pass it on to her; so all she could do was sit tight and wait.

In the meantime she set about clearing out the house. Val returned to help her and Annie quizzed her on what she knew about her mother's affair with Professor Nunce.

'She really loved him you know,' Val said, as if that would excuse her behaviour. 'I don't know how he felt about her but I know your mum wanted him to leave Iris and set up home with her. I could understand the guilt he felt after the accident and why he ended it. It was such a dreadful blow to your mother.'

'Did you know she used me to send messages to him?' Annie said. 'I was caught in the middle not knowing what was going on, why they were both so angry with me.'

'It must have been hard for you, Annie.'

'I had Edward at least,' Annie said. 'And as long as I had Edward I knew I could survive anything.' Until, suddenly, on that spring morning in Cambridge, she didn't have Edward anymore.

'I saw you driving by with him the other day,' Val shook her out of the memory. 'Is he back? Are you seeing him?'

Annie returned her attention to the cupboard she'd been emptying.

'We're catching up on old times,' she said.

Like mother, like daughter, the unwelcome thought intruded. She'd read the rest of the diary — distasteful though it was — and had discerned a pattern, a similarity between her and her mother: the passion for and the obsession with the Nunce men, the waiting around for them only to be disappointed. She didn't want to be like her mother.

★ ★ ★

As the week slipped by Annie still hadn't heard from Edward. There were a number of viewings to keep her occupied and in between the house was cleared, things packed and transported.

Teresa took a couple of pieces of furniture.

'Are you sure about this?' she said as her husband and one of his friends manoeuvred a handsome antique chest of drawers into a van. 'Even if you don't want to keep it, it could be worth something. You ought to get it valued first.'

Annie didn't care; she just wanted to be rid of everything, for every piece was a reminder of the past she wanted to leave behind, especially now she knew about her mother's affair.

She invited Tim to come and take his pick of the rest of it.

'There must be some poor parishioners who'd appreciate good-quality, second-hand furniture,' she said.

'I can think of a couple.' He ran his hand over the smooth walnut of the display cabinet she'd emptied of its china and knick-knacks. 'But you'd be surprised; Chattelcombe isn't exactly a poor area. Some of it might come in handy for the retreat centre if we can find a place to store it.'

'You really think you're going to get The Priory?'

'I have to believe it.'

'You don't have enough money.'

'We've got the gift day on Sunday.'

'Edward will outbid you, whatever offer you manage to make,' Annie shook her head.

'Faith!' Tim exhorted.

'I wish I had yours.' Annie sighed.

'Speaking of Edward Nunce, have you heard from him?'

'Not a word.'

Annie didn't like being reminded of it; it niggled her. Edward had been so keen to see her and, despite everything, she had wanted to see him again. Sometimes she berated herself for still being in thrall to him.

'He'll be in touch Annie. I've seen the way he looks at you.'

She shot Tim a quick glance.

'I think he loves you,' Tim said. He looked as if he regretted it.

'I don't know,' she protested.

'When he does get in touch, perhaps you might persuade him to join us in laying the ghosts to rest at Chattel-combe Priory?'

Something inside her leapt at the thought of that. Surely, deep down, Edward must have been struggling with what he'd done all those years ago. Here was a chance to put it right, to find peace and redemption. But would he take it?

She waited for his phone call.

* * *

It was Tim who heard from him first — indirectly, through the estate agent.

'Edward's put in an offer on The Priory,' he rang Annie to let her know.

'How much?'

'It meets the asking price. Even with the money pledged at our gift day we're still well short. You're right, we can't match him.'

Annie had never heard Tim sound despondent before.

'What are you going to do?' she asked.

'Try and raise some more. Get the estate agent to persuade the vendor that our plans for the house make more sense than his. I don't know, we'll come up with something.'

'Don't give up yet!' she said fervently. 'Faith!'

'I won't. If it's right, it'll be ours.'

But the conviction Tim always had in his voice had disappeared.

Not long after, Edward rang. Hearing his voice brought to the surface so many emotions.

'Annie, how are you?' He sounded his usual bright, confident self, as if he'd only been out of touch for a couple of days, not almost a fortnight.

'I thought you might have forgotten about me.'

'I'm sorry, I've had a lot of things to attend to. I can come down to Chattelcombe this weekend. Can I see you?'

'Edward, there are things we need to talk about,' she said.

'I know. There's something I want to ask you.'

The implication stopped her short.

'We need to talk about the future, Annie.' He spoke into the silence.

'We've got to talk about the past, too,' she said.

'Shall we have dinner at The George?'

he skimmed over her reminder.

It was tempting, but Annie suddenly knew the venue for their meeting.

'I think we should meet at The Priory,' she said.

'Okay, kind of appropriate,' he agreed. 'I'll pick you up.'

'No. I'll meet you there. Saturday. Ten o'clock.' She was giving the orders and it felt good to have Edward follow for a change.

'Whatever you say,' he accepted cheerfully.

He had plenty to be cheerful about, she frowned; he'd won the battle for The Priory, and, judging by his remarks, he thought he'd won her too. Annie knew it wasn't going to be that simple: part of her longed for it, part of her realised too much had happened between them.

'I've heard from Edward,' she told Tim when she bumped into him in the butcher's in the village the next morning. 'He's coming down here this weekend.'

'Good,' he said non-commitally.

'We're meeting at The Priory on Saturday morning. He says there's something he wants to ask me.'

'I'm really pleased for you Annie.' Tim smiled. 'I hope everything works out for you.'

8

Saturday morning was unseasonably grey and overcast — a contrast to the glorious weather they'd been having recently.

Annie was the first to arrive at The Priory. As she strolled up the driveway she saw movement among the ruins and her heart began to pound until the sound of children shouting told her that these were no ghosts.

There were three boys jumping around on the ancient stones, shooting pretend guns at one another. One of them stopped when he saw her.

'What are you doing here?' she demanded. 'Don't you know that this is private property?'

'Do you live here lady?' one of the boys with a cheeky face and wearing a back-to-front baseball cap challenged.

'No, I don't,' she said, 'but the

person who's going to be buying it will be here soon.'

'We're only playing,' said another.

'You ought to be careful. You could have an accident,' Annie warned. 'A little girl nearly died here.'

'Cool!'

'When?'

'A long time ago, before you were born.'

'We're not doing any harm,' said the cheeky-faced boy as he pointed an imaginary gun at her.

What was wrong with children in this country? Annie was still wondering when the familiar sound of Edward's BMW drew her attention and she watched the car do a semi-circle in front of the house.

Edward got out, looking at the boys. 'Oi! Clear off! You're trespassing!'

They took one look at him and scarpered, charging down the driveway, making the sound of gunshots as they went.

'Cheeky sods,' he said as he came

towards her. 'Hi Annie. You're looking great.' He smiled.

'You've put in an offer on the house I hear,' she dispensed with the pleasantries. 'Why didn't you tell me?'

'I was going to tell you this weekend.'

'I found out via Tim.'

'Trust him to get in there!' Edward rolled his eyes. 'Anyway, it doesn't matter. I think my offer will be accepted. I've persuaded Craig to give me the keys for today. Let's go inside. We can take as long as we want this time,' he assured her.

'No Edward. I want to stay out here.'

'In this place?' He cast a glance around the crumbling walls and empty window embrasures.

'I think it's important that we do.'

'Why?' he wrinkled his nose in distaste. 'It'll be warmer inside. I don't know if you've noticed but this doesn't feel like a June day! We can go to our cubby hole, or sit on the stairs — the places that mean something to us. It's important for what I want to say.'

'And so is this place for me,' she resisted his suggestions.

'Annie, Annie,' his voice softened as he moved towards her.

'It's here or nowhere,' she said firmly.

'Okay, okay,' Edward conceded, tucking his hands into the pockets of his jacket.

Annie wondered what he was going to pull out of them; she didn't know if she was ready for it.

'There's something I want to ask you Annie,' he said. 'I made a mistake all those years ago; I made the wrong choice. I knew I was hurting you but somehow it didn't seem to matter then. I took your devotion for granted. I've never found anyone else like you. I think we belong together, that we won't be happy until we admit it. I want you to come away with me.'

His hands were out of his pockets. There was no ring.

'Where?' she croaked through a dry mouth.

'Anywhere you want to go — Venice,

London, New York. We can travel. I've got money.'

'I don't need money,' she said quickly.

'You can take your photographs wherever we are. Let's get away from here, away from the past. Let's do what we should have done back then.'

He took her hand in his, carressed it as he held it against his chest. She could feel his beating heart.

'I've been lonely,' he confessed. 'There have been other women, but I've never found what we had.'

'I was your acolyte. I worshipped you,' Annie said.

He smiled. 'I know.' Then he kissed her tenderly.

'And even though you knew that, you hurt me,' Annie accused as she drew away. 'I even believe you took a kind of perverse pleasure in it.'

'What can I say? I was young and arrogant.' He kissed her again, then nuzzled her neck. 'I need you Annie. I need you to heal me, to make me into a good person. Come away with me and make me whole again.'

It was all about him, even now, not about her. She untangled her hand from his and stepped back.

'I'm not your unquestioning follower anymore, Edward,' she said. 'At one time I would have walked into hell with you, but you destroyed all of that.'

'Annie, let's move on. Can't we forget the past?'

'You say you want me to heal you. But you can't start healing until you come to terms with the past, not run away from it. That's why I wanted to meet you here, in this place. You remember what happened here Edward, don't you?'

'Alright,' he said cautiously. She could tell by the look in his eyes that he was still convinced he'd win her around, that he was biding his time until the inevitable capitulation.

Annie walked away a distance, to the wall of what would have been the old refectory. There were foxgloves growing at its base, a splash of colour against the grey stone, the dry yellow grass and the grey sky. She took a deep breath.

'Did you know that the day Charlotte was injured your father couldn't be found because he was sleeping with my mother?'

Edward's eyes widened in shock.

'That's right,' Annie said. 'They were having an affair. I found my mother's diary when I was clearing out the house. It's all written in there, all the detail.'

It was the first time she'd ever had the upper hand over him, Annie realised. Edward turned to the wall, resting one hand against it while he digested the information.

'It was a shock to me too,' she said. 'I thought you ought to know.'

'Why?'

Because she wanted to hurt him, the way he'd hurt her all those years ago. But more than that, she wanted him to face up to the past. She didn't answer his question.

'I've seen Charlotte here,' she said instead.

'No Annie, it's just your mind playing tricks,' he pushed off from the wall and turned to face her again.

'Don't you ever feel haunted by what happened?'

'It was an accident.'

'You still pushed her. And then we both covered it up.'

'I can live with it. It's not my problem if you can't.'

'Perhaps Charlotte wanted us to come back, perhaps she's drawn us here for a purpose. It does seem too much of a coincidence.'

'Your mother died, I wanted to buy the house — end of story,' he said cynically. 'Come on Annie, I didn't take you for a paid up member of the God Squad.'

'You don't know me Edward. You haven't known me for the past twelve years!' she threw at him. 'Anyway, you were the one who used to talk about the ghosts of people who'd been tortured here.'

'But we were just kids back then,

Annie. I was only trying to frighten you and Charlotte!'

'You talk about healing. This is where it can start, by going back Edward, by coming to terms with what happened all those years ago!' she urged. 'Tim wants to say some prayers here.'

'The vicar?' He turned to face her, staring at her intently. 'Have you told him? Have you broken our bond, that promise you made to me?' His eyes flashed with an anger she'd seen before in the past when his plans had been thwarted, when Charlotte had taken her away from him, when his sister had wanted to spoil his fun. It was as if the man had been replaced by the child. 'Good God Annie, you're my secret keeper!'

'And did you ever care about breaking my trust in you?' she threw back. 'What you did to me that day in Cambridge was so cruel Edward! But I've got over it, I've moved on. And now it's time to finally lay those ghosts to rest, once and for all.'

'I can't believe you'd tell someone!'

'Tim's a priest. It was in confidence. No one else will ever know. Don't you want to find some peace?'

'Peace?' He laughed mirthlessly. 'You're talking like someone old before their time. Life isn't about peace; it's about adventure, challenge.' He suddenly caught her hand and pulled her to him. 'That's why you stuck by me, Annie. You liked the danger, you liked the excitement! Well you can still have that. Come with me!'

At last Annie could see him for what he was — a manipulator. He had to have his acolyte, not her as a person, but what she stood for.

'Let go of me Edward,' she said calmly.

He looked at her, puzzled.

'Let go,' she said again.

'Come on Annie, you want me. You've always wanted me!' His grip was insistent, his voice harsh. She was transported back to that day with Charlotte, remembering how he'd hated to be threatened or challenged, how his sister's declaration that she would tell on him had pushed him over the boundary and resulted in her fall. Was he going to do the same to her? She'd always been a little bit afraid of him she suddenly realised. Now she wished the boys had stayed behind.

Just as she was getting really worried about being out here alone with Edward, a car came up the drive. She was relieved to recognise Tim's Renault. Edward lessened his grip and threw Tim a filthy look as the car came to a halt and he got out.

'What are you doing here?' he snarled.

'Is everything all right?' Tim looked at Annie.

'Everything's fine, go away!' Edward snapped.

'We're finished here,' Annie took advantage of the distraction to free herself from Edward's strong grasp and stepped beyond his reach. 'We're finished Edward.'

He looked at her in disbelief. She

finally knew it was true, but even then she wanted to reach out and help him.

'We're coming back to say prayers Edward. Why don't you join us? I think it will help you.'

'Really? You think it will help?' He sneered. 'I don't think so.'

'Then goodbye, Edward,' Annie said.

He couldn't say the word himself. With a face like thunder he pushed past Tim. Annie watched him walk to his car knowing that she would never see him again.

'I'm sorry for intruding,' Tim explained as Edward drove away in a screech of tyres. 'I wanted to make sure someone was on hand in case things turned nasty, although I'm sure you were handling it.'

'I'm glad you came,' Annie said, relieved, and she threw her arms around his neck and gave him a hug. Tentatively, he hugged her back.

Annie's phone buzzed in her pocket and she drew away — embarrassed now — to take the call. It was Paul from the estate agent's.

'I've had an offer on the house!' She beamed when it was concluded. 'Full asking price.'

'Then you're set to go back to the States,' Tim said.

'Yes, I guess I am.'

9

For the first time in her life Annie felt free of Edward Nunce. It was over, or almost. She'd seen him for who he really was — a manipulator, a coward and a lonely man. Yet she'd still loved him, she'd never deny that. She felt sorry for what had happened all those years ago and for the future he'd condemned himself to.

'It will catch up with him one day,' Tim had said as he'd driven her home after Edward had left. 'These things can only be buried for so long. Underneath his arrogant exterior I think Edward Nunce is a broken man.'

Annie had looked at Tim at her side and felt safe, happy that she was in his car, not Edward's.

It was almost over, but not quite, because Edward was still going to buy The Priory and there was unfinished business to take care of.

'Let's come back here tomorrow, Annie, straight after the church service,' Tim said when she mentioned his suggestion that they say prayers together for Charlotte.

'Just you and me?' Annie asked.

'Of course. I wouldn't betray your confidence.'

Even after everything that had happened, Annie rang The George Hotel when she got home and left a message for Edward to let him know what their intentions were for the following day and that he would be welcome to join them. She didn't expect to hear from him in return, and she didn't.

That night, sleeping in her old bedroom that her mother had turned into a guestroom for visitors who never came to stay, Annie lay awake for a long time listening to the summer rain pitting against the window, contemplating the events of the past few weeks. Her stomach churned over at the thought of all that had happened.

Soon this house would be gone, sold to strangers who would change it and make it their own. She would never return here. She would go back to New York and the past would be gone forever. But where did she belong? If her Chattelcombe roots were severed, if Edward was no longer a presence in her life, where did she belong? Tim had said you had to belong somewhere. Manhattan, work and Jessica seemed such an emotional as well as a physical distance away.

★ ★ ★

The following day after church Annie returned to The Priory with Tim. She was half hoping that Edward would be there after all but they found themselves alone.

It had rained heavily overnight and the thirsty grass was sodden. Surfaces glistened as if they'd been washed clean and made new. The air was clear and fresh with the scent of wet earth. It all seemed appropriate for a new start.

'So what do we do?' Annie said, feeling nervous and slightly foolish.

'I'll read a passage of scripture, say a couple of prayers and then we'll say The Lord's Prayer together,' Tim draped a white stole around his neck; it was his only concession to a uniform for he wore no robes.

'So no chucking of holy water and walking around things seven times?' Annie quipped.

'No.' He grinned.

'Phew!' Annie looked towards the empty windows of the south façade of The Priory's ruins. There were no shadows present today. 'Do you think I can say something first?' she asked.

'I think that would be an excellent idea.'

Annie led the way inside the broken walls of the chapel, close to where it had happened all those years ago. Funny how she couldn't remember the exact spot; time played tricks on the mind. She paused, feeling awkward. Tim waited in silence. Annie cleared her throat.

'Charlotte, if you're here — and I think you might be — I just want to say sorry for what happened back then and for keeping quiet about it for all of these years.'

Annie grew in confidence and as she entered into the moment she even forgot Tim was there. It was just her and Charlotte and she was able to say all the things that had been on her mind for years. It all came pouring out — her blind devotion to Edward and how sorry she was that at times it had led her to neglect Charlotte.

'You were the one to extend the hand of friendship to me and I spurned it so often because I wanted to be with Edward and he demanded that I be exclusive. I'm sorry for the games we played with you, the merciless teasing. There were times when I was horrible and to say Edward made me like that is no excuse.'

She apologised for not being honest about the accident, for keeping Edward's secret. And finally she spoke of her mother and the professor.

'I'm sorry she kept him from you when you needed him most.' Annie felt wetness on her cheeks as that awful day came back to her in vivid clarity. 'I'm sorry I wasn't more of a friend to you. I can see Edward for what he is now. I think he's a damaged person, but he won't ever admit it so he always will be. I'm sorry Charlotte. It wasn't right, none of it was right. You were a good friend to me and I'm sorry for everything.'

Annie choked back a sob as all the pent-up emotion rose to the surface and bubbled out.

'Okay,' Tim stepped in. 'I'll take it from here.'

There was something soothing and reassuring in the way he read and said prayers — no histrionics, no raised voice or wild arm waving; just a calm authority. By the time he asked her to join him in reciting The Lord's Prayer she'd recovered sufficiently to do so.

'I think that's done,' he said at the end. 'How do you feel?'

'Cleansed.' Annie sighed deeply and as she looked around she caught a glimpse of blue and a smile of absolution before the apparition faded into nothingness. Annie knew she would never see it again.

Tim surveyed the ruins and sniffed the air.

'I think everything will be all right now,' he said.

Annie nodded. In that moment, as she knew she'd received Charlotte's forgiveness, she'd extended her own to her mother, for all those years of anger and bitterness and criticism, for a home life and childhood that had been less than nurturing at times. But she understood now — everyone had their own demons to deal with.

'Let's go home,' she said.

She offered him a coffee but he declined.

'I'd really like to stay, Annie, but I've got some notes to prepare for even-song,' he said.

'Do you know, I think I believe again,' Annie confessed. 'After all these years. The way you do it seems to work.'

He reached for her hand and squeezed it.

★ ★ ★

Annie called in at the flower shop the following morning and told Teresa everything that had happened between her and Edward on Saturday — omitting all references to Charlotte.

'So that is it, he's gone?' Teresa shook her head. 'I'm surprised, I admit; I thought he was all over you. I thought you liked him.'

'There was too much in the past that came between us,' was all Annie would say. 'And now I've had an offer on the house I can think about going back to New York.'

'You've had an offer? That's brilliant!

When will you go?'

'As soon as I can make the arrangements I suppose.' Annie hadn't really given it much thought.

'I'll miss you,' Teresa said. 'What about Tim?'

'What about Tim?'

Teresa trimmed the end of a ribbon on a wreath. 'I think he'll miss you even more. He was quite low after evensong last night.'

Annie couldn't imagine why: they'd had a successful outcome at The Priory and he'd seemed cheerful when he'd dropped her back home.

'I think this business with The Priory is getting him down,' Teresa explained. 'He's had his heart set on that retreat centre but he can't get the money together and it seems the vendor is going to go with the better offer. All that effort for nothing. It's a pity really, because we really pulled together to make it happen.'

The bell over the shop door rang as a customer came in.

'Do you want to come around for a meal tonight?' Teresa offered.

'That'll be great.'

'I've got to make the most of you before we lose you.' Teresa smiled before turning her attention to her customer. 'Hello there, what can I do for you today?'

★ ★ ★

Annie walked along the village High Street, her mind awash with a myriad thoughts. Edward Nunce didn't deserve Chattelcombe Priory. Tim was feeling low and he'd revealed nothing of his mood to her yesterday because he'd wanted to concentrate on what she needed; he was always there for her. He'd even come up to The Priory on Saturday because he was worried something might happen to her.

For the first time Annie began to confront the reality of returning to New York. She'd miss Chattelcombe High Street, she thought, as she strolled along it now, looking at the familiar shop fronts. She'd miss the sense of community and the friends she'd made; she'd miss the church group. But most of all she'd miss Teresa and Dylan and Val Linton; she'd miss belonging somewhere.

But there was one thing she'd miss above all these and the realisation hit her like a huge weight. An idea suddenly took hold, an idea so reckless and altruistic that it made her catch her breath. It was ridiculous! Yet somehow it felt right and the excitement of it set her heart racing.

★ ★ ★

'Please be in, please be in,' she muttered under her breath as she arrived at the vicarage. The people she passed on the way must have thought she'd finally gone mad.

She hopped from foot to foot as she rang the doorbell and waited. When Tim opened the door he had a slice of toast in one hand and a mobile phone clamped to his ear in the other.

'I'm glad I've caught you at home!' Annie said breathlessly.

'Jeff, I'm going to have to call you back,' Tim spoke into his phone before flipping it shut. 'Annie, what is it? Come in.'

He was working in the study, the computer was on, papers and books spread out over the desk, a plate of toast and a mug of tea on the side. Annie walked to the centre of the room and turned to face him, a big smile on her face.

'So, it looks as if the retreat centre isn't going to happen,' she said. 'Teresa tells me you can't match Edward's offer and the vendor would rather go with the money than the plan?'

Tim nodded.

'No miracle then,' she said.

'Perhaps God's got something else in mind for us.' He tossed the toast on to the plate, put the phone down on the desk with more care.

'Oh ye of little faith!' Annie beamed.

He looked at her quizzically.

'You know I've sold the house,' she said. 'I think that'll make up your short-fall, enable you to match Edward's offer.'

'Annie . . . '

'No,' she stepped in before he could object. 'I want to do this; it feels right to me.'

'It's your inheritance.'

'Which means I can do what I like with it. Don't worry, I make a tidy living, I won't starve. This is far more important. In a funny way it's like redeeming The Priory.'

'Are you sure?'

'Positive.' Annie was delighted at the look of hope and possibilities on his face.

'Oh Annie!' He half moved towards her. She made up the rest of the distance and they met each other in an embrace.

When he kissed her it was so different to Edward's kisses; it was a giving kiss, honest and pure and committed.

'Annie, I think I'm in love with you,' he said, adding with a chuckle, 'and I don't say this because you've just given me a lot of money.'

She laughed, resting her forehead against his, her hands sifting through his unkempt black hair.

'Me too,' she answered. 'I've thought about what you said about belonging somewhere and today I realised it: I want to belong here in Chattelcombe with you.'

'I never thought, never believed I'd hear you say that,' he almost choked with emotion. 'I was convinced you'd want to be with Edward, and when that was over I thought you'd go back to New York. I didn't want to say anything to put any pressure on you. I fell for you the first time I came to visit before the funeral and now . . . now . . . '

'See, miracles do happen,' Annie said gently. Her lips found his again.

She'd have to believe in them now, because she was part of one herself.

★ ★ ★

Annie looked out of the kitchen window towards the ruins of The Old Priory. All around her work was still going on, making the house ready for its grand opening in three days' time.

It had taken nine months to complete the purchase and finish the renovation. When he'd heard about the new bid Edward hadn't upped his offer, choosing to walk away — it was as if he didn't care anymore. Annie hadn't heard from him since the day of their final parting almost a year ago. He was no longer the unspoken presence in her life; it was finished. He no longer held power over her.

'The painters have finally finished in the last bedroom.'

Annie looked up as Tim appeared. He was grinning. By painters he meant the volunteers from the village. Half a dozen men came traipsing in behind him.

'I'll stick the kettle on!' Teresa called